"Remove

Clare clut

she'd had n

thought he could abscond with her and try to kill her, that was one thing. But to endure the ruin of yet another new gown because of his willfulness, was quite another. "I will not."

"Then I will have my woman tear it from you," he said, nodding to the tall Chinese maidservant who stood in the corner of the library of the quaint Kensington townhouse.

The dark, silent Chinese woman in red flowing robes advanced, and Clare retreated to the wall. As the woman's long-nailed fingers reached for her, Clare shrank into the leather-bound volumes. "I will not have this. It is too undignified."

"Ah, my dearest Clare, dignity is precisely what one does not need when one is dead."

"You mean to kill me?"

His patrician hand cupped her cheek as he raised her face to peer into her eyes. "Never doubt it, my dearest. I wish I did not need to, but I do. You would never forget what I have done and, sorry to say, never forgive it, either."

Clare sidestepped the greedy fingers of the Chinese maid. "Tell me why you did it, and I will do what you ask and come quietly."

"Quietly? Clare, you shrieked so loud in the hansom they heard you in Dover."

"One does not put a gun to a lady's rib cage in midday, sir, and expect the lady to accept it as her due. . . ."

CLIVELY CLOSE
WAIT FOR THE DARK

Ann Crowleigh

ZEBRA BOOKS
KENSINGTON PUBLISHING CORP.

ZEBRA BOOKS are published by

Kensington Publishing Corp.
475 Park Avenue South
New York, NY 10016

Zebra and the Z logo are trademarks of Kensington Publishing Corp.

First Printing: September, 1993

Printed in the United States of America

Dedication

Much of the joy I experienced writing this novel derives from two distinctly different learning experiences in my youth.

My father, William Frederick Leber, taught me by example the finest facets of the German character — wit, charm, sincerity, and gemutlichkeit.

My college professor of Chinese history, Kenneth Folsom, now retired Associate Professor of History of the University of Maryland, College Park, taught me and fascinated me more than twenty years ago with tales of a culture so rich, so intricately different from the Western, that still today I yearn to write of it and help others unravel its lingering mysteries.

It was my valiant, if woefully inadequate, attempt here to inspire others with the essence of a few of these lessons. Thank you.

Acknowledgments

The complexities of describing a dead body do not come easily to most of us, including mystery writers whose sleuths make a habit of tripping over them. For helping this writer — and Clare Clively-Murdoch — analyze this one, I am grateful to my dear sister-in-law Ellen Power, who shared her knowledge and years of experience as an emergency room nurse with me and made this book more viable. Thanks, kiddo! I love ya!

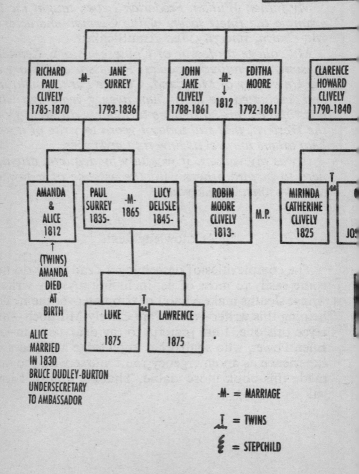

6TH MARQUESS OF SEVERN

RICHARD GEORGE CLIVELY
1755-1815

RICHARD PAUL CLIVELY 1785-1870 —M— JANE SURREY 1793-1836

JOHN JAKE CLIVELY 1788-1861 —M— 1812 EDITHA MOORE 1792-1861

CLARENCE HOWARD CLIVELY 1790-1840

AMANDA & ALICE 1812

PAUL SURREY 1835- —M— 1865 LUCY DELISLE 1845-

ROBIN MOORE CLIVELY 1813- M.P.

MIRINDA CATHERINE CLIVELY 1825

(TWINS)
AMANDA DIED AT BIRTH

ALICE MARRIED IN 1830 BRUCE DUDLEY-BURTON UNDERSECRETARY TO AMBASSADOR

LUKE 1875

LAWRENCE 1875

-M- = MARRIAGE

I͜ = TWINS

ℰ = STEPCHILD

CHART FOR
OF SEVERN

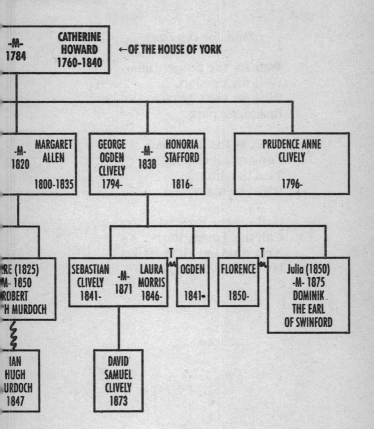

-M-
1784
**CATHERINE
HOWARD
1760-1840**   ←OF THE HOUSE OF YORK

-M-
1820
**MARGARET
ALLEN

1800-1835**

**GEORGE
OGDEN
CLIVELY
1794-**   -M-
1838   **HONORIA
STAFFORD

1816-**

**PRUDENCE ANNE
CLIVELY

1796-**

RE (1825)
-M- 1850
ROBERT
H MURDOCH

**SEBASTIAN
CLIVELY
1841-**   -M-
1871   **LAURA
MORRIS
1846-**   T   **OGDEN

1841-**   **FLORENCE

1850-**   T   **Julia (1850)
-M- 1875
DOMINIK
THE EARL
OF SWINFORD**

IAN
HUGH
URDOCH
1847

**DAVID
SAMUEL
CLIVELY
1873**

Wait for the Dark

Wait for the proper time.
Wait for the dark.
Wait for the Chinaman
Inside the park.

Look at the little man.
Look at his clothes!
Tied in a bundle
Right by his nose.

Call for the Peelers!
Call the *Times,* too!
Next time the killer strikes
He might choose *you!*

One

She will crack the chandelier.

Clare Clively-Murdoch tore her eyes from the shrill soprano standing before her grand piano and glanced up at the crystal pendants shivering in the tumult.

The woman was oblivious. A true *artiste,* she clasped her hands beneath her copious bosom, elbows pointing due north and south, and sucked in a gust of air that almost collapsed Clare's lungs.

The Waterford pendants swayed.

Lady Clare watched in horrified fascination.

Madame LaTour reached higher still. Bracing herself against the curve of the piano, she whipped another stanza to its death.

Clare's chin receded into her neck.

If the woman tried any more bravura in this ditty, she would not only shatter Grandmother's Waterford chandelier to shards, but she would also shower Clare's and Mirinda's guests with a thousand everlasting reminders of the Clively twins' fiftieth birthday celebration.

Gad. Wait until I put my hands on you, Freddie Matheson.

Clare glared at her lifelong friend across the room.

9

He flashed a toothy smile, the bounder.

She sat perfectly still. Perfectly. But she couldn't help grinding her teeth at the next blast. Or letting her eyes fall closed as the soprano's generous bosom heaved heavenward and she hit—and warbled—a high C.

Freddie, you may claim to be my dear departed husband's best school chum, but I swear I am going to draw and quarter you, then serve your gizzard to that parrot Paul brought me. I am going to shock everyone, including Mirinda, with how ruthless I truly am, because not once during the entire torture will I deign to ask why—*in all of Victoria's vast kingdom—you decided* this *coloratura would add the right note to our birthday musicale.*

Clare forced herself to propriety, plastered a blank look worthy of an Adam's frieze on her face, and opened her eyes.

Ah, yes, LaTour was colorful, certainly. Violet dress, hennaed hair, powdered face, and rouged cheeks. She resembled a painted barge. She also puffed like one. Oh, but London loved her. Well, she might have starred in that new comic opera by Gilbert and Sullivan at the Royalty, but she certainly did not sound well in Clare's parlour.

No, not at all. LaTour sounded like a homesick parrot.

Clare's eyes slid to the somnambulant feathered creature her cousin Paul had bought her as a birthday present.

"From the splendours of Peru," Paul had announced as he pecked Clare on the cheek, then turned to Mirinda to deposit a King Charles spaniel pup in her hands.

Totally stalling the receiving line, Mirinda and Clare had stood there, speechless. And fuming. Animals were certainly one sign of approaching senility. Was Paul saying that when one had no children, one must pass the days until Judgment catering to *animals?*

Clare groaned and narrowed her eyes at the parrot perched on a swing inside its tall, oval wire cage.

Gad. What did one do with a bird?

Couldn't take it for a stroll or a carriage ride. Couldn't curl up with it or stroke its fur or chuck it under its chin. Pfff.

"My dear," John Newhall leaned closer to whisper in her ear, "are you quite well?"

She smiled benignly.

"Absolutely." She smiled at him fully, appreciating how his gray eyes fired in response. Gad, how she liked fires like that.

She'd not seen a fire like that in . . . oh, five years at least, not since that American railroad tycoon had swept into London, sat at Clare's right during Prince Bertie's dinner party at Sandringham, and regaled her as no man had since her husband Robert's untimely death.

Now, here was John Newhall, newly promoted at the Foreign Office and newly attentive to her. She liked that. It gratified her that at her age—oh, gad, why not admit it?—at her *advanced* age, she could still find excitement in being courted.

Mirinda could. No, not true. Mirinda *did.* Clare did not even have to look at her twin sister to feel what she was experiencing at this most amazing moment.

Gus stood behind her, his long-fingered hands flexing surreptitiously now and then. Did he restrain himself from skimming Mirinda's naked shoulders to affirm physically, poignantly, *I am here?*

Mirinda had scarcely breathed since he had walked in the door two hours before. Walked in uninvited and filled Clare's vestibule with his commanding, blond, Germanic power. Walked in just as the receiving line had dwindled to naught. Walked in with his friends, Frenchman Charles Beaumont, Englishman John Newhall, and the Portuguese emissary Petro Saldahna, and apologized for his intrusion.

"Dear Gus," Clare had stepped in when Mirinda, for once in her life, could not find her voice, "you are never an intruder!"

Clare curtsied to the man who was His Highness, the Grand Duke Gustav von Frey, the prince Hessebogen of Hesse-Kassel. Then she hugged him close and kissed him on the cheek, opening the path to the similar greeting he could then offer Mirinda. But, true to his princely heritage—and his passionate nature—he did not merely hug Mirinda nor kiss her cheek, but took her hand in chivalrous homage and pressed his lips lingeringly to the back of her hand.

Mirinda swallowed, and when she spoke she croaked, then cleared her throat. "Your Highness," she put herself together enough to curtsy, "we are delighted you came. You know you never need an invitation here."

His copen blue eyes danced merrily while he explained how he had arrived only that morning on a special mission from His Imperial Majesty, Kaiser Wilhelm, to Her Royal Majesty, Queen Victoria.

"When my friends Charles Beaumont, John Newhall, and His Excellency Saldahna told me they were invited here this evening, I prevailed upon them to bring me with them."

His expression was jovial, polite, a tad indifferent.

But Clare knew better. She could see the way his hungry blue eyes devoured her sister. The way his body leaned toward hers. The way his words shook Mirinda to the core when he announced he would remain in England indefinitely. Clare saw the way Mirinda absorbed it all as if it were some child's fairy tale.

Clare pinched Mirinda's waist. "We are honoured to have you, aren't we, Indy? You must introduce the Grand Duke yourself, my dear. And I must sit down," she lied. "Terrible bout last winter, and I am not quite recovered."

"Es tut mir leid. I am so sorry to hear that, Clare."

Then, because all the Clively clan and their friends had arrived, Hopkins shut Clare's front door and signaled to her that the reception line was closed.

Gus saw the butler's look, and he promptly took one of Clare's hands and one of Mirinda's, allowing both sisters to lead him into Clare's parlour. There, he seated Clare in a comfortable chair next to John Newhall, and after Indy's introductory duties were done, Gus took up his hovering position behind Mirinda, the woman who had always been the love of his life.

Clare sighed. Just to look at them reminded her of the one man who had meant everything to her. But with Robert, she had had five years. With Gus, Mirinda had had none.

Clare could actually feel the aching void constantly felt by her sister. All these years, Clare had watched and waited, hoping things might change for Indy and

13

Gus. But that was like calling back the dead. It was impossible.

"What did you really think?" John Newhall was clapping for the soprano and smiling knowingly down at her.

Clare remembered herself and applauded the woman.

"She was extraordinary."

He snorted. "Never breach etiquette, do you, my dear?" He winked.

She suppressed a grin. "I must confess I love your cavalier attitude, John."

He cocked a handsome brow. "I must confess I love your ability to rally—continually, I might add."

The guests began to mill about, and a warm buzz filled the air. Hopkins and the two young footmen, Connery and Burton, passed among the people with flutes of champagne. Clare took one, as did John.

He touched his glass to hers, allowing his dove-gray eyes to say more than his words. "Best wishes on your birthday, Clare. You always were the only woman I ever called extraordinary. You have a joy of living that shows."

"Thank you, John. That's very kind—"

"I assure you, Clare, I am not being simply kind."

No. What he was being was very direct. And she loved it. She tilted her head and really looked at him.

At fifty-five, John Newhall was a very attractive man. Gray hair, gray eyes, clear skin, and a long, lean body. He was a man she could find appealing. He was also a man she could find intellectually stimulating, because he was witty and wise and had managed to build a career in the Foreign Office in spite of his basic irreverent nature. Now with his recent promotion to the status of Gus and Saldahna, John took on another aspect that permitted him to court a woman: He had a future.

"John, I—"

"Clare, forgive me, we have known each other for so many years and I—"

"Well, frankly, John, I never thought that you . . . that is, I never thought that I . . ." She snapped her mouth shut. "It's been years since I . . . Help me, will you, John?"

"I would love to. I have wanted to proclaim my admiration of you for a long, long time, Clare. I have always felt—how shall I say it?—comfortable, compatible with you. You are so special, so very rare, and I have always dreamed that one day you and I might have the opportunity to discover more mutual pleasures than shared friends and shared weekend parties."

"John, I must tell you how . . . how flattered I am." *How ecstatic. How embarrassingly gratified.*

"Good. I want you to be flattered, Clare. I told myself before I came tonight that I would try to make you see my intentions. I hope I haven't completely skewered my chances by being so bold." He cast his eyes to his champagne, and when he raised them, he seared her with silver desire. "I like your laugh, Clare. *Your* cavalier ways. I want to call on you, Clare. Say I may. I want us to be more than friends. Say it, Clare."

"I would like you to call, John."

He took one of her hands and squeezed it. "Thank you, Clare. Tuesday afternoon?"

She was nodding, imagining how it would be if once more a man would put his arms around her, bind her to him, rob her breath with kisses. . . .

15

He was smiling. "You will come out with me. Tea and the new Assyrian exhibit at The Henworth, how does that sound?"

"Breathtaking."

He was considering the line of her lips. "That's what I thought, too." He brought her hand to his mouth and kissed it. "Now, lest I spoil my victory by asking for more, I will escort you in to supper."

He stayed at her side and she enjoyed his attentions, until all together, three of the new tenants in the Close appeared before her to bid her good night. The Brewsters from Number 6 and Mrs Lee Davenport from Number 20 took their leave politely. Charles Beaumont then nodded to John, whose eyes went to their friend Saldahna.

"We must go, Clare." He took her hand and kissed it. "I am delighted to have been a part of your celebration."

"I am delighted you came, John."

"So am I, so am I. Good night, my dear. You need not see me out. I will thank Mirinda before I go. Until Tuesday at four." He smiled and winked at her before he turned for Mirinda.

She watched him go. Tall, trim in his tailored black tuxedo, he cut an elegant figure. Personable and pleasing, John kissed Mirinda's cheek and turned for the door, where Connery draped his cape over his shoulders, and Hopkins handed over his top hat, gloves, and ivory-handled walking stick. Then, with a open palm, he allowed his friends Beaumont and Saldahna to precede him out into the night.

"My, my. John Newhall. Not a bad catch, I'll say . . . I *do* say, Clare? Clare?"

Clare turned to stare straight into the laughing visage of her Aunt Prudence.

"Got yourself a suitor, do you? Hmmm. About time, too. You have needed a man for—"

"Aunt Pru! Shame on you. Drink your brandy."

She did. Drained the snifter to the bottom, smacked her lips, and winked at her niece in exact imitation of John Newhall.

"You could do worse, Clare. Most widows who have loved as deeply as you loved Robert do make fools of themselves over some man at one time or another."

Clare grinned. "Aunt, are you talking about *me?* Or are you writing one of your plots?"

"Yes, I am talking about you, and no, I am not writing one of my plots, because I have already written this story." Pru was chuckling and absentmindedly stabbing Clare's cartouche carpet with her cane. "Sold rather well, too, I might add. Wrote it in '64. *Mourning Becomes Martha,* it was. Did you read it? Where *is* your man with the brandy? Answer me. Did you read it?"

Clare was trying desperately not to guffaw. "No, Aunt, not that one."

"Well, you should. Yes, here, Hopkins, give me a real portion, will you, not a daub? There, that's good. Thank you." She sipped a little of her brandy, rolling it about on her tongue in thought. "Very nice brandy. French, isn't it? You've chosen well. But then, you have good taste, Clare. Very good taste. You are an attractive, mature woman, Clare. You have suffered with that illness from this winter, but your eyes look clearer and your hair has come back from lankness. You are still too thin. You always were very well endowed and . . . now, now, hear me out. Whatever it

17

was that felled you didn't rob you of your complexion or give you gray hairs. Of course, your eyes did water a bit too—"

"Aunt Pru," Clare laughed, "must you discuss my physical maladies—which I am attempting to improve, I might add—in a room full of my guests?"

"Now, now. Do not become ruffled, my dear. I was simply trying to make the point that you are a lovely, if slightly older woman, beyond society's concern for a little dalliance here and there. So if John Newhall seems to fill Robert's shoes, I say, after all these years—"

"Please, Aunt Pru," Clare pleaded, returning a smile to Robin and his fiancée Sarah Mattingly across the room. "No one will ever take the place of Robert."

"There's no harm in enjoying others, Clare. No harm. Robert, if he were here, God bless him, would want you to take your happiness where you find it. If Newhall appeals to you, my dear, I say get on with it. Robert Murdoch was not a man to truss you up in life, so why let some unrealistic sense of loyalty to him cut you off from whatever joy you can find with another man?"

That was precisely Clare's line of reasoning, but she had been brought up in a society that did not condone such confessions from women, even *mature* women. So she smiled at her irrepressible aunt and murmured her agreement.

Not only was the subject opened now, but the wound was laid bare. And as she circulated amongst her family and laughed with her friends, she was remembering five years of bliss. And excitement. Agony. And loss.

And every glance in Mirinda's direction brought

vivid reminders of exactly what she had lost. Her breathing slowed. Her chest constricted. She knew she could blame it on this winter's malady, but in her heart, Clare knew she was coming down with a strong case of fresh grief.

She stood beside Mirinda and bid the rest of their guests adieu. She supervised Hopkins as he began to clear the remains. Saw the parlour furniture rearranged. Put the violin stand just so, covered the harp. Then she swirled about and stopped. On a pivot, Clare tore herself from the sight of Gus murmuring good night to Indy, and she dissolved through the French doors onto the portico.

She collapsed against the brick wall and forced the night air into her lungs. She fought for sanity, fought off the visions.

Gad. This has happened so frequently over the years, I should be able to deal with it better.

She had learned a few things in the past twenty-five years. She had learned to breathe deeply and to think of something else, anything else. To avoid thoughts of Vienna, where she'd first met Robert and Indy had first met Gus. To avoid thoughts of waltzing with Robert in St. Petersburg, laughing in their bed in Naples, greeting their guests in Cairo and Bombay, Hong Kong and Shanghai.

Ahhh, God, what torment.

She fled the portico for the gazebo. Recently finished by the workmen who had transformed the entire estate into the Close, the gazebo had been designed by Clare. Its odor of newly cut and painted wood wafted about her on the clear night breeze. The rain that had prohibited them from hosting the musicale here, as they had planned, had vanished. In its place, Clare

19

was left with wild self-recrimination that she had designed this gazebo in just the same manner as her memory of one particular gazebo in Shanghai.

She gazed about. Gad. She had even ordered it painted in bright white gloss. What had she been thinking of?

She knew. She knew.

Clare touched a miniature azalea she had spent hours pinching and shaping, just as the Zen master had taught her decades ago. She leaned over the rail to admire the new spring growth on the rhododendron bushes. The willow sapling was doing nicely, despite all the rain they had had lately. Then she sat upon the wooden seat to consider the peonies, which budded beautifully, and the lilies, which sprouted straight and strong around the bed. She was glad she had taken the gardenias into the conservatory to blossom, their perfume having filled the air at supper tonight.

She had selected them all, by herself. Gotten Indy's approval for the plan and Paul's help to secure the rarest species from India and China. She had even planted them all, by herself.

She had created this, despite Indy's oft repeated doubts. She had insisted, pressed for this scenery, this expression of one place, one time in her life when every moment throbbed with beauty and serenity.

Oh, yes, she had created this as a living memorial to what she and Robert had shared.

As the realization hit her, she smiled.

She breathed more easily.

The willow bent in the breeze and Clare knew she was bending, too. Acclimating.

She grinned and rose to take a tour of the grounds.

Benson and his crew had done a truly admirable job of clearing away the carriage house. Their work had been halted temporarily, of course, by the discovery of that poor baby's body in the chimney, and they had all taken a bit of time to recover from that tragedy.

She walked down the newly paved alley that ran behind the Close residences. Only four of the townhouses were let to date, and all of the tenants were reputable people. Mr Michael Brewster, M.P. for Lancaster, and his young spouse in Number 6. The Scotsman, Her Majesty's Royal Navy Capt. Gerald Fitzhugh and his wife, in Number 8. Mr Devon Attenborough, shipowner, with his wife and three children in Number 10. And the widow Mrs Lee Davenport, formerly of Shanghai and Tokyo, in Number 20.

They had each attended tonight's celebration. Indy and Clare had thought it an appropriate moment to bring them together socially. They had mingled well, even to the point of including the beautiful half-caste Lee Davenport in their conversations. Judging from the darkness of their houses, each had retired now.

Calm once more, Clare wandered around Scarborough House on Indy's side, pinching off dead buds from phlox and pinks, ever careful not to dirty her gown.

The night was sweet now. Soft.

She crossed the circular drive and headed for the park, which gave the Close an expanse of green. New gas lanterns, with new ornate glass domes, lined the drive and lit her way as she continued to find new gardening work. With all the preparations for the musicale, she had been neglecting her gardens. She must come out tomorrow and do a thorough job.

As she checked the tulips and surveyed the new

growth on the boxwoods, Clare began to hum one of the tunes Madame LaTour had sung, despite the woman's rendition. She noted that the dead growth on the cloudy mass of gypsophilia, which backed the iron fencing and secluded those in the park from prying eyes, needed trimming. Making a mental note for tomorrow, she worked her way toward the statue of their father. Beneath his bronze gaze, she smiled up at him.

"Would you believe Indy and I are half a century old, Papa?"

She made a face.

"No. I don't, either."

She bent to examine a patch of pink impatiens and at once stood back.

Now, why would there be yellow amidst the pink? It was not intended, nor should it be there.

She looked closer. It was not a flower. The bright color wound its way directly to a body.

A body sprawled among the flowers.

A—a *dead* body.

A partially *nude* body.

A—a *castrated* body of a young man.

A young and very handsome Chinese man!

Two

Clare knelt by his side among the damp impatiens. Oblivious to the damage she might inflict on the silver silk gown she had had designed for this evening, she placed her hands carefully on either side of his chest and let her palms sink into the wet earth.

Ear to his chest, she heard nothing. Three fingers half an inch under his nose, she felt nothing. Applying the same three fingers to his carotid, she pressed. His skin was so chilled, she jumped. He had no pulse.

What did she expect?

She stood up again, and the shock to her system subsided and transformed into reason.

Scanning his form, she now registered *why* he was lifeless. He had bled to death. The telltale black evidence between his legs had pooled atop tiny pink flower petals and dried in the night air.

Hands to her mouth, she swallowed back bile.

Poor man. He had come to this country seeking . . . something . . . and had found only death in a park. Beneath her father's statue.

She leaned over him again. Sprawled in death's throes, he still clutched himself with the lax fingers of one hand, where the life had pumped out of him. With the other hand, he had crumpled the tunic and vest on his chest. These garments had bloodstains.

23

Some were drops of blood. Others were larger, darker circles. One stain, at his right rib cage, drifted down to the earth. A few were smudged fingerprints, as if he had been grasping at himself, trying to stem the flow.

He hadn't succeeded. His complexion, waxen even in the gaslight, gave proof of that, as did his dark drooping eyes, the pupils fixed and dilated.

But the yellow scarf intrigued her most. About six feet long, it wound around his throat and over his broad chest, to splay across the flowers. Thick silk in rich buttercup-yellow, it extended from his throat to just beside his mouth, and clearly, from the teeth marks, his assailant had stuffed the scarf into his mouth before committing the vilest act one man could do to another.

Poor man. She needed to cover him but she halted, her hand in midair. From what she had learned from her stepson Ian's training at the Yard, the best clues to solving a mystery and finding the evildoer came from the scene of the crime. She knew she should touch nothing else. Disturb not even one pink petal.

Scooping up her skirts, Clare cut across the grass and hurried up the brick stairs, banging the huge brass knocker on her front door.

No one came.

Had they gone to bed?

Had Gus left?

She didn't think she had been outside as long as all that, but perhaps she had. She backed off the porch and looked up at black windows. All tight and tidy. Clare refused to wake up the entire Close with her knocking, and she absolutely refused to be a party to spreading such a dreadful tale, particularly among

24

their new neighbours. The only way to get in quickly and quietly was to go round to the servants' entrance on the ground floor. If she knew the ever-fastidious Hopkins and Louise, both would have all the staff still up and about, clearing the buffet supper and washing the china and silver, putting everything in its appointed place before the fires were lit tomorrow morning.

She fled round the house on her side so she wouldn't have to dodge the dust bins and the kitchen gardens. Scurrying down the basement steps, she reached for the kitchen door, when it flew open.

"Ouff!" Clare barked as she thrust out one hand to stop the door from hitting her in the face.

"Lady Murdoch!" Connery, one of the footmen, blinked bewildered eyes at her.

"Yes, it's me." She threw him an apologetic look and ran through the door, leaving him with a sack of garbage in his hands, staring after her.

Inside Pence's domain, Hopkins halted in mid-stride, a huge tray of brandy snifters teetering from the shock of seeing his mistress belowstairs.

"Mum! I—"

"No time, Hopkins," she said as she passed him. "Sorry, Pence," she added to the startled cook as she pushed through swinging doors to the servants' stairs, then up into Mirinda's side of the house.

"Mirin—?"

She stifled her call. What if Gus *were* still here?

Silently, she ran up the stairs to the ground floor and made for Indy's drawing room. She knocked once, then thrust open the door and drew it shut in one swift movement. The gas had been turned down. The room was empty. Clare took two steps and glanced into the Butler's Pantry as she rapped once and opened the door to her sister's dining room. Not in either place. On a jog, she rounded the corner and took to the hall. Her chest hurt and she had to sag against the wall a moment to catch her breath. With measured steps, she went to Indy's library and client waiting room. She walked into the room and swung the door wide so that she might peer into Indy's studio just beyond.

There, in the dim yellow and sepia mix of moonlight and gaslight, sat her sister in her favorite chair. She sat stoically gazing out her broad windows. Perhaps Gus *had* gone home. Thank God.

"Indy! Thank God you're here."

"Clare!" Her sister twisted about, her hand to her chest. "My God, you gave me a fright. I thought you had retired long ago. Gus wanted to say good night and we couldn't find you. Where have you been?"

Clare stumbled two steps forward, clutching the doorjamb while she tried to recover her breath.

"Outside! I was outside! Oh, Indy. Come with me. I hate to tell you, my dear, but I am afraid—" She gulped. "Indy, I have found something quite awful. Quite . . . awful."

Mirinda was out of her chair in a second, her hand combing the light brown hair from her sister's forehead and feeling the brow for fever. "What is wrong with you? Short of breath again? Overexerting yourself when the doctor said you must be calm? Come sit down. What have you found? Not another baby, I'll wager. Sit there."

"No, Indy. I don't want to sit. We—"

"Oh, my God, Clare!" Mirinda fell away from Clare in horror. "What's happened to your gown? It's

26

crushed and stained. It's—"

"It's rain or dew." She didn't glance at it, didn't think about her next words. "It could be dirt or blood."

Indy chortled. Clare had always been less conspicuously outrageous than her older twin, but no less prone to pranks and little deviations from society's precepts. But the way Clare's gray eyes bored into hers told Mirinda now was not one of those times. She moved closer, put one hand to Clare's forearm, and stared at her sister.

"*Why,* dear Clare, would you have blood on your gown?"

Breathing more slowly now that she was with her sister, Clare twined their fingers together and began to lead Indy down the corridor. "Come with me, dear. Out to the Clively bench, near Papa's statue. Among the flowers, Indy. Among the flowers, I have found a dead man."

Indy dug her feet in. "Clare, you can't be serious!"

Clare spun her head around. "Oh, yes, my dear, I am quite serious. We have a dead Chinese man in front of the Clively bench. And he has been horribly mutilated! You won't believe how terribly, terribly butchered!"

Mirinda covered her mouth with both hands. "Awful. Awful." She stooped closer and looked into his blank eyes. "He is cold, you say?"

"Very."

"Not surprising. The life has been cut from him."

"No. You know gelding does not kill a horse—or a man. If it's done right, that is."

27

Mirinda turned wide eyes upon her twin.

Clare knew explanations were in order. "An artery must have been cut. When this procedure is done correctly, only a few minor blood vessels are severed. This, as you can see, was a quick job. A nasty one. Besides, if he had suffered through an adequately done operation, he would certainly not have been able to walk. Not for days. But he would have had time and the energy to crawl to someone in the Close for help."

Indy arched both brows at her sister.

"Veins seep. They ooze. A cut to a vein gives a person time. To an artery" — she drifted off, remembering one terrible incident at the Czar's court — "a person has only a few minutes."

"We can't leave him here."

"And we can't be tramping about, either."

"Ian."

"Precisely."

"I'll get him."

"Bring a lantern, too. But don't let the staff know. I fear they'll up and leave if they hear we have another dead body in our midst."

Mirinda nodded, picked up her skirts, and crossed the park and the drive. She didn't bother to explain that the staff would have to know about this body sooner or later. So would the new tenants.

She shuddered and shook off the chill as she rounded the house on Clare's side, headed for Ian's private stairs, still under construction.

She picked her way up the stairs, avoiding sawdust and ill-driven nails in the posts. She would speak to Benson about shoddiness tomorrow.

Once up the stairs and in front of Ian's private

door, she knocked softly three times. Before she could do it again, his man Drummond swung the door open.

The man-of-all-work had turned up the gas in his hall lamp, and he blinked sleep from his eyes as he secured the sash of his quilted red flannel robe.

"Lady Mirinda?" He peered at her and dragged a hand through his wild brown hair. "What's amiss, milady? It's late, and I—"

"Yes, man, I know. Please get your master for me. It's late, but it's urgent."

"Come in from the chill, then, will you, milady," he entreated, his thick brogue coming out with his solicitous care.

She stepped into Ian's tiny vestibule, waiting as Drummond padded down the hall and around the corner.

Ian appeared before her almost immediately, his mahogany hair mussed, his green eyes black with sleep and curiosity. He gathered his robe about his tall, solid body as he squinted at her in the dim light.

"Aunt? What are you doing up? Drummond said—"

"No time to explain, Ian." She walked forward to press her fingers into his forearm and gaze into his eyes with a pleading look. "Please, put on a pair of trousers and come with me."

He straightened. Seven years in his father's regiment meant he not only slept lightly but awakened instantly. Expediency was the order of the day, *any* day, for a man on Her Majesty's watch. He knew how uncertain the world was. He didn't need explanations. The blank look on his aunt's face was enough. He pivoted and made for his bedroom.

Within scarcely a minute, he was back, an old pair of charcoal trousers and an ivory wool sweater encasing his broad six-foot frame.

Mirinda nodded, lips folded tightly together.

He opened the door and held it while his aunt swept past. He knew better than to press for answers to minor questions when she obviously had major ones on her mind.

"We'll need a lantern," she whispered to him at the bottom of the stairs.

"Right," he whispered back. "Stay here and I'll get one from the shed."

She watched him move quiet as a cat through the grass, along the path to the rose garden, and round the gazebo. She clasped her hands together and inhaled the night air.

God, what a night! She had had nightmares over it for weeks. Nightmares over what it meant to turn fifty, what it symbolized. What it indicated she was about to endure and what it showed she had never possessed. A night she had faced with definite distaste. And then she had found herself faced with a unique opportunity—and another dead body.

Ian took her elbow with one hand, a lit lantern in the other. "Where do we go?"

"The park."

Clare stood where Mirinda had left her, hands clasped, head bowed, eyes riveted on the man amidst the flowers.

Ian's emerald eyes followed his stepmother's and he sucked in his breath. Raising the lantern high, he crouched by the body and examined it inch by inch for

30

long minutes. Finally, he rose and stood between his stepmother and aunt at the foot of the body.

"Been dead two or three hours, perhaps more. Hemorrhage was the cause, of course."

"From an artery?" Mirinda queried.

"I would say so. Otherwise, he would have been able to crawl to get help."

Mirinda looked admiringly at Clare. "That's what your mother said."

"He could have cried out, though," he pointed out.

"No," Clare shook her head sadly. "The poor man's assailant stuffed the yellow scarf in his mouth."

"Quite right, Mother." Ian smiled at them each in turn. "Come back to the house, both of you. I must get the authorities."

"We can't just leave him, Ian," Clare objected.

"Everyone's in bed, my dear. Worn out from your party. No one will come out here."

"Still, we can't leave him so . . . so *exposed*."

"I understand, Mother, but we don't want to disturb too much, you realize."

"Do it quickly, then. I'll stay with him."

"No, Mother. It's not good for you to be out in the night air. You've been ill. Come with—"

"*No,* Ian. I am staying here until his poor body is taken away to wherever you take them. His ancestors will not even consider accepting him until his body is properly ministered to. Until such time, I will remain here." She softened her virulence a little. "Merely get me my shawl. I'll be fine."

He knew when she raised her voice that way she was determined. Helpless, Ian glanced at his aunt. Mirinda shook her head at him.

"I'll get you both your shawls."

He was two steps away when he spun around.

"Mother, explain to me what you just said about his ancestors."

Her sad eyes flicked up to his inquisitive ones. "It is what he would believe, Ian. What he would believe and what I must respect. His body needs to be properly washed and clothed for burial before his ancestors will even consider accepting him into their pantheon. Horribly mutilated as he is, they may not accept him at all, even if he does have someone attending his body." Thinking Ian meant to argue with her more, she repeated, "I will stay here."

"Yes, yes, I know you must, Mother. But I need to know why you talk of his ancestors. He—"

"He is Chinese, Ian. From his clothes, to his eyes, to his body's shape and build, he is Chinese."

He had his mouth opened when she continued, "I *know* he is Chinese. His tunic and trousers are of a twilled cotton I would recognize in a moment. They are from the factories up the Yangtze River. So is the style. You wouldn't remember, of course. You were too young. But they are the loose pyjamas I saw every day of our two years in the Treaty Ports."

"But many Orientals wear such garb."

"Perhaps, but he is Chinese."

"Not Japanese?"

"No, the Japanese are shorter of limb. Plus those who are posted here now dress in our western style. The men cut their hair as our men do. Short to the scalp.

"Whereas, this poor gentleman is—what would you say? Ten or eleven stone? Five feet six? Not as tall as some Han Chinese, certainly, but tall enough. He has fine, straight hair, to his chin. Not as black as the Japanese. He is well-muscled, obviously well-fed, athletic." She frowned. "Not like some of the *kuli* laborers who slave and then starve on a bowl of rice a day."

Mirinda moved close and circled her arm about her sister's waist. "Don't think about such things, dear. You have been disturbed enough for one night."

Mirinda couldn't bear to think of Clare coming down once more with the illness that had confined her to bed for the winter. She knew how affected Clare could be by empathy, and she didn't want to see her twin relapse from a combination of chilling night air and a sympathetic ague.

"No, no, Indy." Clare stared into her sister's worried hazel eyes. "Don't you see? No, no, of course, you don't." She focused on the man again. "But I do. Yes, I do. He is not a *kuli*. Look at his hands. Except for a few new callouses, they're smooth. Look at his nails, short but clipped. Clean. If he works at the East End docks, he is no ordinary *kuli*." She took a step forward. "He's not a mandarin, either. His nails are not that long. But even if they were, what would a mandarin be doing in London, England? The Dragon Throne hasn't even condescended to send us an ambassador yet, let alone a lesser *literati*."

Ian put up one palm. "Wait, wait, Mother. I can't —"

"But his nails . . . something about his nails. They are too perfect. They might once have been long. Yes. They might have been. Perhaps he had to work to come here. Of course! He had to work. At the docks, on a ship. How else would he get here? And working with his hands, his fingernails broke. Yet afterward" — she gazed at the dead man admiringly, piti-

33

fully—"the teachings of a lifetime made him return to a perfect manicure."

Ian stood, hands dangling at his sides. He had memorized her every syllable. "Don't move," he murmured. "I'll return with your coats."

Three

The cacophony resounded up the servants' stairs through the sturdy walls of Scarborough House. Clare had known it would. It might be Sunday, but there was no peace on earth here.

As soon as the Peelers had finished interrogating them a few minutes ago about last night's events and the poor man in the park, Pence began clanging pots and pans in the kitchen. The scullery maids began screeching. The footmen, Connery and Burton, took to the alley to smoke their pipes. The two upstairs maids, Dora and Patsie, frantically grabbed up their feather dusters and attacked every nook and cranny in the four-hundred-year-old house. Hopkins and Louise were probably huddled away in their parlour, staring at each other and biting their lips white rather than letting the rest of the staff know they possessed an emotion called fear.

Of them all, only Clare's maid, Colette, shrugged in grand Gallic resignation and asked if *Madame* wished a lighter shawl now that she and Mirinda had decided to take their elevenses in the warm June sun streaming into the conservatory.

"Thank you, Colette, but I don't think I need one at all. It is a brilliant day."

"As you wish, *Madame*." She gave a little inclination with her pretty head. "I will go now to Lady Prudence, *oui?*"

"*Oui,* Colette. There, there, do not look frightened. Lady Prudence does not bite. Bark, yes. But do not fear. Entice her with the idea of snails for luncheon. Pence can't stand the stuff, thinking them naught but garden pests. Of course, you shall supervise her butter and garlic sauce so it will be edible. But run along to Lady Prudence now. Mind you, tell her nothing of what has transpired here."

"Yes," Mirinda added. "We don't want her to think we've another family mystery on our hands. Although, God help us, we are not certain of anything except that. Or are we?"

Clare shook her head at her sister. "What we may have are friends who ignore us for giving their names to the police. And tenants who move out."

An income that dwindles. Further scandal as the *Times* and every other newspaper drag the Clively name into sordid territory. Again.

Colette arched her delicate brow at her mistress's novel breach of etiquette to discuss family matters in front of staff. "*Oui, Madame. Au revoir.*"

Mirinda reached across the octagon-shaped oak tea table and offered Clare her third cup of tea. "Ah, youth! She takes it all so very well. I envy you your ability to keep her when I'm left with eighty-year-old day help."

"It isn't her youth that makes her immune, Indy. You know how they say the French are nonplussed. Colette wrote the bible on blank looks. So you see, her stoicism has absolutely nothing at all to do with my actions. And your having to make do with Ida and Lettie Smart is only because younger maids won't put up with your shenanigans." At Mirinda's arched brow, she nodded her head vigorously. "Don't give me that Howard eye! You know it is true."

"Half true."

"True enough." She laughed. "Really, Indy, stop! I cannot drink all this tea you are pouring down me."

"Drink it. And eat these gingersnaps. They're good for you. Scour away any tendencies to another illness. You were up most of the night. Drink it all."

Clare accepted the cup and a crispy cookie with good humour. "So were you up all night, and I do not see *you* floating away on a barge of tea. My dear, really, if I drink any more of this, I will have to take up residence outside my W.C., and remove my crinolette *and* my bustle for speed."

"Remove what you like, Clare. The Peelers won't return today." Mirinda chuckled as she poured her own second cup of lapsong oolong. "I want you well."

Clare had not looked well in several months. A late winter cold had lingered, seeming to sap the strength from her bones. Her usually fine, light brown hair was lustreless. Her gray eyes had lost their usual spark of humour and were often pain-wracked or watery. Her soft, well-endowed figure had thinned and was beginning to look more like Mirinda's. Though Colette plied her needle every night to take in the voluminous number of clothes Clare owned, it mattered little in the long run. Dimity, lace, or organza—like the pale peach day dress Clare wore today—all hung on her body like made-over bags. Yet today, perhaps because of this new puzzle laid out in the park, Clare's cheeks were sparked with more colour than they'd had in weeks and her eyes danced with renewed enthusiasm. For those reasons alone, Mirinda decided that this new trouble was worth the aggravation.

She grinned at her twin. "I want you well enough to continue to tell the police exactly what they need to know."

"It was rather funny, wasn't it?" Clare sipped her tea, then placed her cup and saucer on the white wire-framed table to her right, pushing the fronds from the top of a voluminous fern.

"Hilarious," Mirinda confirmed as she broke into her poached egg. "Sad."

"Yes, quite. I understand, though. I really do. So few English know much about China."

"Yes, but it's both countries' faults."

"Our relationship with the Chinese throne is muddled with misunderstandings. Few Westerners speak their language and fewer still write it. Only now that the Dragon Throne has lost numerous trade wars to us do the Chinese begin to study our languages and our cultures. Both sides appoint men who are woefully unprepared to negotiate politely for what they want. We Westerners, seeing ourselves as militarily—and even culturally—superior, tend to pound the table and demand. But the Chinese view themselves as divinely ordained to rule the world and tend to consider every minute detail to its absurdity. The result? Westerner and Chinese advance not a bit."

She sighed, took another bite of the cookie, and put the rest aside. She truly did not have much appetite.

"If our own government doesn't understand the people with whom they deal each day, how can we expect the average citizen to do so? The police are not to blame for their ignorance of the Chinese, because those in power who should know more know very

38

little indeed."

"I thought you did a marvelous job of setting them straight." Mirinda, who had finished her egg and toast in the interim, sat back into the soft Turkish cushions of the settee with her own cup of tea in hand. "I thought the Dawes brothers would break their hands writing it all down! The look on their faces!"

"It was nothing to their superior's. What was his name? Fleming? Indelicate man. Not my type of Peeler. Too uncouth. Calling that poor man a China-man, as if he had no right to a proper appellation. Then, asking me if I went out last night because I were meeting someone or if I made a habit of such excursions! And where, pray tell, was I headed? Pfff."

"Don't trouble yourself about him. He listened to you. He didn't like it that you knew the victim was Chinese and not Burmese or even Indian. Good God, anyone knows that a Indian has entirely different bone structure and skin tone."

"As we said, Indy," Clare inhaled and bit back the discomfort in her chest, "some know so little. It's shocking, really."

"Hello, Mother, Aunt Mirinda!"

Ian came in, jaunty even though he had been up all night, rousing the police and bringing them round with the mortician's lorry close behind. Through it all, he had solicitously cared for his stepmother and aunt and still managed to make his usual meeting with his superior at nine. He looked strong, healthy, and none the worse for wear, but Clare eyed him as she had every morning of their life together.

His rich red-brown wavy hair was ragged from the habit he had of running his fingers through it when he was involved in a deep puzzle. She had caught him at it dozens of times when he was a child studying for his lessons. Police work had only aggravated the habit. But his features were not puckered in worry, as she had feared. His clear green eyes looked slightly tired, but not frightfully so. And his square chin was clean-shaven . . . probably had had a quick fix at the station. And as usual with Ian, his mouth was upturned in a slight smile that crinkled the corners of his eyes so delightfully it drew the attentions of every girl within his purview. Satisfying, that. So much like his father . . .

Nevertheless, Clare asked, "How are you, Ian?" offering him her cheek to kiss.

"A little the worse for arguing with Bloom," he said as he kissed his aunt and sat beside her. "Any more of that I might filch, Aunt? Missed breakfast and I'm starved."

"Certainly." She sat up, pushed the plate of cookies and another of sweet rolls toward him, and reached for the extra cup Hopkins always added to the tea tray just for insurance. "Your mother and I were just discussing this morning's interviews with the police. What does Bloom say?"

Clare smiled when Ian dragged a hand through his hair and accepted his cup of tea.

"Well, by now I think you know Bloom."

They both nodded at him and waited while he gobbled down three cookies and a roll, took a few good sips of his brew, unbuttoned his vest, and sat back.

"Impervious to anything or any *one* who has theories. *No conjectures are allowed, Murdoch! None! Facts, that's all we want. Deductions come later.*" Ian rolled his eyes.

Clare shook her head. "I am afraid I don't understand. It is a fact that the poor man is Chinese. That he has the build, the clothes — "

"Yes, Mother, but until we can prove it, Bloom says we cannot simply take the word of a private citizen who discovered his body in a park."

Ian did not repeat Bloom's phrase verbatim. If he had, his mother and aunt would have risen off their seats like levitating swamis.

Your mother, Bloom had hooked his arms akimbo as he faced Ian, *says he is a Chinaman!*

Chinese, Ian had corrected him, eyes straight ahead, voice flat.

Very well, Murdoch. Chinese! What does your mother know? Hmmm? And how? And why?

Though Ian had explained how he and Clare had accompanied his father when Robert Murdoch had been posted in Hong Kong and Shanghai in '54 and '55, Bloom disbelieved a *woman* could absorb so much of the atmosphere in a Treaty Port that she could hold forth on racial types so easily or so quickly. When Ian attempted to explain that Lady Clare Clively-Murdoch was no woman to sequester herself inside the foreign settlements and ignore the world about her, Bloom listened but gave it little import.

We will have to find evidence, Murdoch. Evidence. From the scene. From the body. Then, we shall deduce where next to look. First, let's see what the doctor tells us about how the fellow met his death, shall we?

The doctor had concluded his examination of the body less than an hour ago. His report went simultaneously to the Dawes brothers, who were the local constables on the Clively Close beat, their superior Fleming, and Detective Superintendent John Bloom, since the latter had requested notification as soon as it was finished. Because one of his probationers was involved in the discovery of the victim, Bloom felt it imperative he involve himself personally in the investigation, *for form's sake,* he had said. But Ian knew it was more than form. It was *vital* that Bloom establish for himself — and anyone else at the Yard who might ask — how and why one of their young recruits in training had stumbled on a murder victim outside his family's home.

As soon as Bloom skimmed the postmortem report, he told Ian about its contents, and Ian asked if he might come to assure his mother and aunt that things were progressing nicely. Bloom had grudgingly agreed because, Ian was sure, the man had a basic belief that women needed coddling more than they needed courtesy or consideration.

"The doctor at the Yard confirmed quite a few of our suspicions. The man was killed by hemorrhage. A jagged cut of the femoral artery that runs near the groin. He had other wounds, too, cuts from a short knife. None of them could have killed him, though. In fact, the most serious were two jabs to the rib cage. But even those were not as serious as the cut to the femoral."

"Knives," Clare shuddered.

Mirinda sighed. "I thought we had seen enough of knives when deLisle was killed."

"Yes, Aunt. This attack was very similar, it seems."

"What kind of knife?" Clare asked him.

"Short," he repeated. "That is the only thing we can conclude. The only puncture wounds were the ones in the midsection, and those were approximately an inch deep. All other cuts are superficial."

Mirinda took another sip of tea. "Are there any other injuries to the body? Broken bones, bruises? . . ."

"No broken bones. A few bruises from the scuffle in the park, but most were purple or yellowed, which means the injuries happened days ago."

"Where?" asked Clare.

When Ian started in surprise, Clare knew she had to clarify her question.

"Where are the bruises on his body?"

"Legs. Calves, really. Three or four. But on the upper shoulders, there are many. It's as if he were carrying water on one of those balance beams the peasants use throughout the East. But, of course, we know he wasn't doing that here."

"No," said Mirinda, "but he was obviously carrying something."

"God knows," Clare offered, "he had the physique to carry anything."

Ian put down his cup and saucer. "The report says he was five foot seven. No distinguishing marks. No old wounds. No old scars. But a healthy man of perhaps twenty-five or thirty years, with pronounced musculature of the upper and lower torso."

"Athletic," said Mirinda.

"Therefore," Clare asserted, pleased that she had been correct, "he was well fed, from birth and through his young life. Not like your *kuli* or rice-bowl convert from the rural *Han*, whose development is stunted by poor rations from the cradle. Yes, our gentleman was just that, a gentleman."

"Then what was he doing in London working like a

43

coolie?" asked Mirinda.

Ian shrugged and reached for a piece of toast.

Clare's thoughts drifted. "And why would a person attack another with a knife and then emasculate him? It does not make sense."

"Mmmm," Ian mused as he munched on a piece of toast and swallowed, "unless he thought the cuts to the rib cage were lethal and then emasculated him."

Mirinda sat forward. "But why emasculate him at all? It's a difficult thing to do—fell a man, open his legs, and keep them open while he reaches behind . . . well, you know what I mean."

"Absolutely, Indy. Hard to accomplish. A man would have to be extremely strong. Which brings us to another point. Our attacker *is* a man, wouldn't you say? No woman could have held him down, unless there were more than one woman. Ooh, there's a horrid thought. A group of women doing that to a man. But if there had been a group of women, wouldn't we have known? Wouldn't we have heard? Or . . . oh, dear God, I never thought of this . . . but wouldn't our guests have seen something? Seen someone? Seen *the* someone?"

Ian and Mirinda stared at her, their faces frozen with the horror of such a thought.

Four

Clare had been talking to herself, thinking out loud, so she did not hear Ian and Indy say, simultaneously, *Oh God! Of course!* She just kept rattling on.

"So our assailant was a man. Armed with a short knife. And strong. As strong as our Chinese gentleman. No, no. Stronger!"

"Yes," Ian said. "Whatever he did, however he accomplished it, he did it all *very* quickly."

"Right you are," Mirinda nodded. "We had too many guests for him, whoever he was, not to notice, not to fear discovery at any moment."

Ian agreed. "He had to move swiftly and think quickly. Very quickly."

Mirinda moved forward in her seat and narrowed her eyes at him. "He had to be absolutely ruthless. Far more than any man we have ever known, ever conceived in our wildest imaginings." Her chilling tone forced even she to move to some more rational level. "Perhaps Hopkins saw something odd as he tended the front door."

"Possibly."

"But let's be positive, if we can. Clare, reach over and pull the bellrope for Hopkins."

Their ever-prompt, ever-officious butler appeared in minutes. Stiff as a corpse, he stared straight ahead, his gloved hands at his sides. Clare let her eyes wander to Mirinda's, where she read the same conclusion as her own: He was outraged, terrified, chagrined.

"No, mum," he shook his head at Mirinda. "I don't recall anything amiss last night. I told the police the same. Yes, I was opening the door to the guests, but I was not focusing on the park, as you might well imagine."

"Well, then," she rejoined, "perhaps Burton noticed something. He was outside directing the carriage drivers to the rear."

Hopkins started to speak and then thought better of it. Instead, he turned on his heel and returned in a moment with Burton.

Tall and physically fit, as footmen were required to be, thirteen-year-old Burton was also extremely good-looking, with black hair and blue eyes that made girls turn to stare at him. It was no wonder, of course, because with all that devilish appeal, he was also affable, cheery, Welsh to the bone. And today, as one might expect, he was uncharacteristically nervous.

He cast his eyes to the tiled floor.

Mirinda spoke softly. "Burton, we know you were outside last night, directing the coachmen round the drive to the alley. Can you tell us if you noticed anything odd?"

"No, milady, I didn't."

Clare sat forward. "No one walking there?"

"No, milady, I didn't."

Ian tapped his fingers on the armrest of the settee. "Where were you standing as you directed traffic, Burton?"

At this requirement to speak more than a few words, Burton swallowed audibly. "At the foot of the front steps, Mr Murdoch."

"Nowhere else?"

"Uh . . . no. No, sir."

"You didn't go around to the other side of a coach for any reason?"

"No, sir. Everyone got out at the left of their carriage, sir, to enter the front door."

Ian raised his dark brows at his mother and aunt as if to say, *Well, that's that.* But Clare frowned. There was something about Burton's attitude. That slight hesitation. The way he lowered his eyes. She wasn't at all sure *that* was *that.*

"Thank you, Burton," Mirinda smiled at him. "You may leave. You, too, Hopkins. We appreciate your cooperation."

"You are welcome, mum. If I might add a thing, mum?"

"Yes, Hopkins. What is it?"

"The police, it seems, asked each of the staff the same questions. I thought you would like to know that none of us noticed anything amiss last night."

"Thank you, Hopkins."

The butler was visibly relieved, and he turned to push Burton ahead of him. But the footman had already scurried to the door. Hopkins's head snapped up and his charcoal eyes clouded with anger. Burton had just made a serious breech of deportment, Clare knew. And she could imagine the scene when Hopkins had it out with him.

But what Burton had done . . . the hurried exit from their presence . . . only confirmed her suspicions that he knew more than he was telling. Or that he was somehow involved?

My God, what a thought!

But what did they know about Burton?

He was so young, so new to their establishment. He had applied for the job after he'd seen an advert in the *Illustrated*. Hopkins, like his wife Louise and anyone else who looked at the boy, accepted the young man on his smile and open demeanor. Burton knew how to charm. He was Welsh, of course. But that hardly credited. And, of course, he couldn't have had much contact with Chinese immigrants in the tiny Welsh mining town he'd come from. Nor had he had much chance here in London. But did she know that for certain?

Inquiries would have to be made. Through Hopkins and Louise, for a start. Clare shuddered. She did not like the task of spying on her staff, and she certainly liked less the thought that somehow . . . No! Impossible.

Wasn't it?

When Hopkins had closed the conservatory doors behind him, Mirinda finally spoke. "That told us a little."

Clare hemmed a bit. She did not want Indy or Ian to know the whole of what she suspected, lest they take matters into their own hands. The poor man had been left for her to discover. She had more proprietary rights to solving this thing than Mirinda did. It was Ian's job, of course. But he was still only a probationer. And no one . . . no one . . . had had as much experience with the Chinese as she had. Certainly, no one thus far had shown *any* familiarity with the customs. So she thought only a *tiny* prevarication could not hurt.

Clare agreed with Mirinda, adding, "Now we know that last night, Burton saw nothing. We have no examples of how observant he is normally. I have never asked him to perform a task that required acute devotion to detail. Have you, Indy?"

"No. Certainly, he does his work well. He is efficient, quick, courteous."

Ian shook his head. "And very quiet."

Mirinda huffed in frustration. "But he would have noticed this deed being done. How could he not?"

Ian agreed. "God knows how long it takes to actually accomplish such a thing as this."

"And the perpetrator had to be fast, don't you think?" Clare asked them both, rhetorically. "Yes, fast and sure. We had too many people coming and going. And all of the carriages would circle from the alley where their drivers were waiting, back up the front drive, then down and around the park. With all the comings and goings, the murderer—" she choked on the word she had avoided using, "the murderer would have little time to do his worst."

"But evidently," Mirinda said above the rising din of several yapping canines near the front of the house, "he had enough time."

The three of them looked at each other in turn before Ian reached for his vest pocketwatch. "Well, speaking of time, I am afraid I must return to Bloom's protection."

"Convenient," murmured Mirinda.

"Expedient," said his stepmother, then smiled at Mirinda. "He is obviously leaving us to do the honours alone with Aunt Pru."

"My dears," he was grinning as he stood and spread both hands wide, "I am a working man."

"Yes, yes," Clare shot him a smile. "Kiss Aunt Pru on your way out, dear."

"Why, where is he off to?" snapped the white-haired, straight-backed, tiny lady who tapped her cane across the terrazzo, her three Yorkies yipping at her feet and one lone King Charles spaniel puppy romping close behind.

"Back to the Yard, Aunt." Ian bussed her on the cheek, then winked at his stepmother and Aunt Mirinda. "I came home for an early lunch."

"Yes," she clamped her mouth together. "Odd, isn't it, that that man Bloom would let you out to play in mid-morning so early in your probation?"

To that, Ian had little of substance to respond. He only knew he had to remove himself. He would not subject himself to the scene about to unfold here as his stepmother and aunt told Pru about the man in the park.

"Yes, yes. I must run." He made a hasty exit.

Aunt Pru sank immediately onto the high-backed chintz-covered white wicker chair she always favoured.

"So," she arched one white brow and peered at both her nieces. "Come, come. What is it?" She flicked imaginary specks from her impeccable maroon and mauve silk faille day dress.

The two sisters checked each other's eyes, uncertain who would like the duty.

The woman tap-tap-tapped her cane into the terrazzo. "Now, now, don't fill up my dance card and then deny me the waltz."

Tap, tap, tap.

"Shall I enumerate? I see I must. You know I write each morning until noon, even on Sundays. You both are usually invited out to dine with friends. I have never been invited here for luncheon—for which you,

I see from that tray, obviously will not be hungry, since you have had elevenses. Therefore, my dearest nieces, why did Colette come round to invite me to dine on snails, *which,* incidentally, I know as well as you that Pence hates to the point of a screaming fit? Hmmm?"

Napoleon, Josephine, and Marie Louise settled at her skirts, snapping at the small spaniel who sniffed at them mercilessly.

"Stop!" Pru thudded the cane on the floor, and the three Yorkies shut their little jaws. But the spaniel knew only he had friends, and he sat back on his haunches to bark a baby's tale for their ears.

Clare cast an inquisitive eye to the sleeping, nodding parrot in the tall cage. Did this animal sleep night and day?

The puppy barked on.

"Quiet!" Pru leaned over and ordered the spaniel.

He snuffled and then returned to his monologue, unperturbed by her magnificence.

"Ahhhh!" Pru raised her face to the wisteria climbing across the glass-domed roof.

Mirinda chuckled and leaned over to scoop up the animal, who kept Pru from her facts.

"Sorry, Aunt Pru. You must be quiet, Chuzzle." She settled the puppy in her lap and petted his taffy and cream fur. "That's a good boy."

"Chuzzle?" Clare and Pru asked simultaneously.

"Well, yes. Chuzzlewit was appropriate, I thought. He kept me awake most of the night with his snuffling and I thought Dickens would have had someone like this fellow in mind when he created the creature." She chucked the puppy under his chin, and he nuzzled down into her blue and white foulard skirts with a

51

sigh.

"Ha!" crowed Pru. "If I were you, I would be awake all night for other reasons!"

At Pru's implication of impropriety, both Mirinda's and Clare's eyes popped.

Mirinda was the first to recover herself. "Really, Aunt Pru. Gus—"

"Don't *really, Aunt Pru* me, Indy. And don't take it obtusely, either. You know me better than that. After all, do remember I was there the first night you laid eyes on the Grand Duke, Prince Hessebogen of Hesse-Kassel. Such a romantic name. I must remember to create one like it for my next book." She ignored her nieces' groans and continued with her itinerary of the times she had met the inestimable Gus. "Let me see . . . Ah, yes . . . I was in Vienna when you waltzed with him the first time and in Cologne when he revealed he was engaged to be married. And how I tried to console your inconsolable soul! I was in Paris with you when you saw him seven years ago. And I was here last night when he walked through Clare's front door. So don't bother to tell me, by voice or by gesture, that you were awake through last night because this dog missed his mother or couldn't stop up his runny nose. *I* know better."

"Yes, of course," Mirinda murmured down to the dog, "I was . . . utterly . . ."

"Yes," mused Pru, "weren't we all?" She curved a brow at Clare. "So, why am I here? What is your news? Has his dear, saintly wife departed this mortal coil? I could only pray. And how long is he here? Days, weeks? For the Kaiser, no less. I am not surprised, I must say. Gus has always shown himself to be the diplomat *par excellence*. Bismarck would not know how to shine his shoes were it not for Gus's teachings. I wouldn't be surprised if Bismarck replaces the current German ambassador with the one star in the new German Empire's firmament."

"No," Mirinda broke in to Pru's litany.

"Pardon me?" Pru insisted.

"No, Aunt. Gus's wife is not dead. His . . . his personal life has not changed. He administers his duchy as he always did. But his duties to the German Empire have changed. He is Bismarck's special emissary to Whitehall regarding colonial affairs. And he will be here in London indefinitely."

Pru took this news with aplomb. "So . . . the love affair continues at much more comfortable—or is it, uncomfortable?—proximity."

Mirinda was out of her chair, pacing the tile like a madwoman, the dog clutched to her chest. "He is here. That is the only thing I can imbibe at the moment. Do not, please, do not censure me or him. We have not *done anything.*"

The word *yet* hung in the air like bright laundry.

Clare froze. Was Pru the same woman who had encouraged her with John last night? Yes. Aunt Pru knew that Robert was a once-in-a-lifetime *amour* whom Clare had loved madly. Clare could not lose her head over another man the way she had lost it over Robert.

But Mirinda? Mirinda felt the very same passion for Gus that Clare had felt for Robert. And Mirinda had never been able to satisfy her appetite for him. Add that to Indy's tendencies to flaunt rules when she needed to, and Pru might fear the worst. But whatever Mirinda did, Clare knew her sister possessed a wide streak of sanity.

Clare sought to ease the pain for her twin. "Aunt, Gus has rooms at the Langham Hotel. The German Embassy retained the suite for him. He told me last night he has his personal and his diplomatic staff with him and—"

"He will not rent a house on the Close," Pru stated.

Clare could not decipher if this were a statement, a question, or a warning.

Mirinda swirled around to face her aunt. "No, Aunt Pru. He will not rent a house on the Close."

Pru inhaled deeply and smiled for the first time that morning. "Well, now. I am at ease. But then, I remain curious. Why, pray tell, am I invited to luncheon with snails on the menu?"

Five

She stayed to lunch.

She stayed to tea.

"I thought she would stay the night," Mirinda said as she sank against Clare's front door.

"She is concerned," Clare confirmed. "But not as badly as before." Without asking if Mirinda wished to discuss Pru's thoughts privately, she led the way down her hall toward her drawing room.

When they got there, both sank into matching Restoration chairs before one of the two fireplaces. By mute mutual agreement, they sat in silent communion for many moments and then quite suddenly spoke at the same time.

"You first," said Clare.

"No, you," said Mirinda.

Clare lolled her head against the high chair back, eyes trained on the low flames of a June evening's small fire. "*I* am shaken by this second murder. I was, certainly, last night. But the terror cleared quickly and reason stood close behind. It was as if a curtain went up and there stood" — she waved a hand — "cool objectivity."

"I know what you mean. I feel the same."

"Why do you suppose that is?"

Mirinda looked at Clare, her mirror image with the

lighter brown hair and the softer eyes of gray. She raised both brows. "We are inured to murder?"

"Oh, Indy!" Clare hooted with outraged laughter. But when she stopped, she became introspective. "You are right, of course. Finding the baby's body seemed a nightmare."

"And it was a godsend that we could discover the truth after all those years."

"We saved our family's good name."

"No one else could have done it."

"Excuse me, miladies," Hopkins entered with Chuzzlewit in his arms, "Burton has walked the dog, mum." He looked at Mirinda. "He seems content for another twenty minutes or so. What shall I do with him? Take him to the kitchen for the evening?"

"No, no, Hopkins. Give him to me."

"And, if I may inquire"—he handed the squirming puppy into Mirinda's cooing care—"what are miladies' plans for dinner?"

Clare checked Mirinda's hazel eyes before responding. "Nothing. We have eaten our way through today's troubles with yeomen's appetites. Tell Pence she has the evening free."

"Thank you, miladies."

He did not leave.

"Yes, Hopkins? Was there something else?"

"Yes, Lady Clare. Quite a few things." He licked his lips.

Unusual that he needed so much prodding, Clare thought, and she smiled at him in encouragement. "Yes, go on."

"Mr Murdoch sent word around that he will be quite late this evening. He wanted you to know not to expect him."

"Thank you, Hopkins."

"Also, what with Lady Prudence visiting this afternoon, I have not had a chance to ask you about a certain matter. In light of the Peelers . . . I mean, the police coming here this morning and the body of the dead man in the park . . ."

"Yes, yes, Hopkins. *What?*"

"I wonder if there are any special words you wish me to convey to the staff, Lady Clare?"

"Yes, please tell them Lady Mirinda and I are grateful for their cooperation with the police and that we hope they will continue to do so."

"You think they will *return?*" He was appalled, his bushy brows knit tightly, his dark eyes stormy.

"Most likely," said Mirinda as she stroked Chuzzle's head.

Clare cleared her throat. "Investigations are long processes, Hopkins. New clues popping up all the time. Sometimes it is necessary to review not only one's thinking but the facts. You ought to know that from . . . from . . . from the last time," she finished lamely.

"I see," he muttered.

"What else bothers you, Hopkins?"

"Well, mum . . ." He swallowed once, twice, and yet again.

Clare waited.

"What, if anything, should we tell the other staff in the Close?"

Other staff? Clare stared dumbly at him for a moment. The aftershocks of this second earth-shattering murder in their midst began to roll through her system. Without looking at Mirinda, she knew her sister felt the same tremours.

57

Staff did much to assure the calm, efficient running of any household. But while they waited on their employers, they hobnobbed among themselves. Creating their own pecking orders and their own friendships, they also nurtured their own gossip. Some of it was about themselves; much of it was about their employers. And like all gossip, it became riper and rounder with each telling. Staff could start a "tale" that soon became fact to many. Staff could raise one up or cast one down in one swift, indifferent wag of a tongue.

"Tell them the truth, Hopkins. Tell them I found the poor man in the park. He was hideously done in. I fetched Lady Mirinda and Mr Murdoch, who then went directly to the police. What else would you tell them, Hopkins?"

"Exactly, mum. But Mrs Attenborough's upstairs maid was in to tea this afternoon with Mrs Brewster's. Mrs Brewster's maid, Linda, visits Louise because she is her niece."

"Yes, Hopkins. We know about Linda."

"Well, mum, Mrs Attenborough's upstairs maid was very upset. She heard about the fact that the victim was an Oriental person and wondered if he wasn't here in the Close to rob us. I told her that the Close was a perfectly respectable enclave and that never had any thief wandered anywhere near Scarborough House, but you know how insistent some people can be."

"Yes, I do. What else?"

"Well, mum, I thought you should know, mum, that . . . well, mum . . ."

"Enough!" urged Mirinda. "Spit it out, man."

"The word among staff in the Close is that Mrs Davenport is running a very poor establishment at

Number 20. People seem to come and go at all hours of the night."

"Oh?" Clare felt her hackles rise. The familiar prejudice of the Westerner against those of other so-called *lesser* cultures made her want to grind her teeth. "And how does Mrs Attenborough's upstairs maid know this if she herself is indoors by ten o'clock when their man usually locks up the house?"

He swallowed hard. "I did not ask, mum."

Clare closed her eyes and inhaled. "It is not your fault, Hopkins. I simply cannot abide such breaches of reason." Particularly in cases such as this.

"I have one more issue to resolve, mum."

Her eyes went to his.

"The bird, mum. The parrot which Lord Severn brought you for your birthday present, mum. What am I to do now with him?"

Him? How did one discern the gender of a bird? Gad. Clare eyed Mirinda's adoring, adorable puppy and wondered what Paul had been thinking when he bought her a useless, godforsaken parrot!

"I have no idea what to do with him, Hopkins. I may ask my cousin to take him down to Severn House with him. The bird should like Lord Severn's greenhouses, I presume."

"Yes, mum. But I thought you would like to have him with you while you talk. We had him in the kitchen this afternoon after I cleaned out his cage, and he seems to listen."

"Does he? Interesting. The only thing I have seen him do thus far is sleep!" She glanced at Indy, who suppressed a trembling grin. "By all means, Hopkins, bring in the bird."

He returned with the long wire cage in hand, setting

59

it atop her octagonal reading table in the far corner. The bird, true to form, slept soundly. Pfff.

"Thank you, Hopkins." She waited until he had closed the door behind him, before turning to her unusually quiet sister, who petted her dog and stared into the fire. "So, what did you think of Aunt Pru's suggestions?"

Mirinda raised her eyes to Clare's and blinked. "What suggestions?"

So, Clare had been right. To Mirinda, thoughts of murder paled beside thoughts of Gustav von Frey.

"Oh . . . oh, yes," Mirinda recovered on an embarrassed smile. "Sorry, my dear. Aunt Pru. Yes . . . well . . . I think she is correct when she assumes that the world will call on our doorstep tomorrow morning once the *Times* and the *Tatler* and the *Illustrated* spread the news. We can count on the *Times* to keep some propriety about it, but I am not so sure of Ann Billings Wentworth's versions for the other two newspapers. You know how she was when we found the baby's skeleton. Eavesdropping on us, black as coal!" Mirinda smiled and her hazel eyes were admiring. "But she was tenacious. And most helpful. Perhaps if we send round an invitation to her tomorrow to come and hear the whole story, she will write what she must and her editor will dismiss it afterward as a job well done."

"Hmm, that is the least of it. I do wonder what our friends thought when Fleming and the Dawes brothers went round questioning them today? We have heard from none of them."

"I doubt the police managed to see them all. The Dawes brothers did not call at Aunt Pru's until well after three, and when they found she was not in, they left word they would come tomorrow at ten."

"Which means some of our friends and family will discover the tale from the newspapers tomorrow." Clare shuddered. "Not a happy prospect."

"I will be frank, Clare. I do not think our family or friends will blink an eyelash over this. They know us and care for us. Not one person who was here last night doesn't tolerate us for all we truly are. Quite honestly, it is our new neighbors about whom I worry most."

"I know, Indy. If they react poorly, all our hopes and preparations—"

"*And* all our prospects will be gone!"

Clare inhaled deeply. "I know Aunt Pru gave very specific warnings about commenting on the incident, but Indy, I disagree with her on this. I do not think we can afford to let this go by without some sort of discussion or acknowledgment."

"Aunt Pru would have you ground up for haggis if she thought you would ever dare acknowledge another murder on the grounds."

"I know. But she need never know, Indy."

"I suppose not." Mirinda's gaze drifted to the fire as she absently stroked the snoring dog.

"What do you think we should do, Indy?"

"Think? About what?"

Clare sighed. It had been exactly seven years since she had had to prompt Indy like this. Seven years since their trip to Paris—and the last time Indy had been within arm's reach of Gus.

"Should we call on our new neighbors to politely discuss this incident in the park?"

"Oh, my dear. I am not so sure about that." Mirinda raked a hand through her coif. "I—I have appointments tomorrow. Two sittings, one at nine, another at ten o'clock. Then, I am invited out to luncheon. The Italian *charge d'affaires* wonders if I might consider a trip to his country. He wants me to take a few photographs for an Italian scientist who has categorized criminals by cranial formation."

Clare hooted. *"What?"*

"Lombroso is his name. Cesare Lombroso, and no, he is *not* a candidate for Bedlam. I asked. Believe me, I asked. I am going to luncheon simply to learn more. I am fascinated."

"Will you take the commission?"

Mirinda shrugged and patted Chuzzlewit. "I don't know." She was frowning. "It would mean a visit to the Continent."

Ah, yes. And now was definitely not the time to travel to the Continent, when, for once, Gus was here and not there.

"Well, then," said Clare, "I shall call on them alone and give them your regards."

"Please do. I really do not know if I could keep my mind on pleasantries, considering all that has happened." Indy's eyes pleaded and apologized at the same time.

"I understand completely, my dear. I will go alone but speak for both of us."

"Thank you. You are so dear to me, Clare." She reached across to grasp her twin's hand and squeeze it.

"And you to me, Indy." She wanted to say more. She wanted to say, *Beware, be happy, be assured I will always care for you no matter what happens.* But she didn't. Indy would find such sentiments superfluous. Instead, she let her eyes and her heart do the talking.

Indy rose, her lashes attempting to conceal suddenly frightened eyes. "Forgive me, dear. I think I will withdraw. It has been a grueling day."

Clare knew the look Mirinda wore when she craved solitude. "Don't apologize, Indy. Do what you must."

With the puppy in her arms, Mirinda hastened from the room.

Clare watched the closed door a very long time before she realized she was brooding. Brooding over the murdered man in the park. Brooding over their neighbors' reaction to him. Brooding over Indy and Gus. . . . Pfff. If there were anything she loathed in a person, it was brooding. Brooding and whining.

Well! She rose from her chair and went to her desk, gazing beyond the doors out to the gazebo. She hadn't visited there at all today. But tomorrow she would. She would prune and pinch to her heart's content. If there were such a thing anymore. . . .

She got out of bed, careful, *very* careful of how she laid her foot upon the floor. No one was beneath her bedroom at this hour of the night—or morning, rather. But she couldn't afford any slipshod behavior that would give her away. She must ensure no one—*no one* would ever know she had left the house tonight.

She had planned it all so carefully. The time. The place. The note to him. Her clothes. Especially her clothes.

Black as the night. Blank as her hope. Dark as her fear.

She threw her nightgown aside, donning her chemise, drawers, one petticoat and old mourning dress, ignoring the need for corset and bustle and all the other fripperies that rankled her on vital occasions such as this.

She put on thigh-high black silk stockings and secured them with rolled garters. She tied on serviceable shoes.

She brushed and combed her hair, then lifted it high to pin it. No, she would not. She'd let it hang down her back. What did it matter if he saw her so? She was not impressing him with her style or her wit, but with stark realities.

She buttoned the dress high to her chin and long past her wrists, then reached for the tiny hat with the full face veil. The one she had worn for the last funeral. The last death.

She peered at herself through the black mist of the veil and wondered if this were another funeral she was about to attend. Another death she was about to witness.

The horror of it rose in her throat and snagged her breath. She closed her eyes against the terrible confirmation of it and sagged against the dresser.

She had to do this! Had to! Must! Always!

Oh, God! Why? Why was it always this way with her? Doing her duty. And his.

Because the world is not kind, her father had told her.

He had not told her the world could be brutal. No. He had left that for her to learn by herself.

She squared her back, grasped the black cape she had dug from the trunk this afternoon, and swirled it over her shoulders and the hood over her head. She made for the door and the hall. Carpeted, the stairs gave no evidence of her footfalls. Neither did the first floor hall as she headed for the front door.

At the first set of doors, she quietly pushed through. At the second, she paused to reach down inside her dress pocket to pat the key, which she had filched from its place on the foyer table less than an hour ago. She couldn't go out without coming back in. She slowly turned the key in the master lock and winced as it made a scraping sound.

But it opened, and she closed it swiftly behind her. Flush against the aged brick, she surveyed the condition of the Close at the ungodly hour of two in the morning.

The gas lamps burned low now. Patches of fog drifted here and there, but in all, it was a clear night. Not a good night to meet someone secretly.

No one else thought so, either. All the houses were dark, with only the Attenboroughs' gaslight burning, turned very low throughout the night.

She hastened down the front steps and tiptoed along the circular drive, keeping to the hedges for security and concealment. At the foot of the drive, she turned left onto Scarborough Street and there she stopped.

The street was empty. Although at more regular hours it was filled with the residents of the fashionable Georgian townhouses, at this hour no one appeared.

She took a ragged breath.

The black carriage was parked where she'd told him to bring it. One horse stood, blinders on, serene, its warm breath rising in gusts in the cooler night air. With two small lamps on either side of his seat, the driver nodded, asleep at the reins. No one else was about.

She gathered her courage as she gathered her skirts, and she ran to him. God, she ran and ran. . . . Hadn't she always run to him?

The sound of her footsteps on the cobbled street made the coachman lift his head. The horse snorted. The black carriage door swung open.

She reached the step as one long-fingered hand was extended. She grasped it, and the hand pulled her inside. She was safe.

She sank into the warm velvet squabs with wild relief, brushed away the hood, and tore off the tiny hat and absurd veil. The coachman must have closed the door, because her companion had gone quite still.

Into the shadows of ebony night, she searched for him. He sat, his round, yet sharply boned face barely visible to her. He said nothing, letting her set the tone, the pace. She saw how he breathed deeply but not evenly.

She drank her fill of him. Having been deprived of his presence for so long, she now consumed his every feature, however dim, however forbidden. Stray beams of gaslight and moonlight conspired with her to examine him.

He was a hulking figure of a man. Formidable. Intense. With that old fencing scar on his left cheek, he could even appear menacing. But the smart dark suit and crisp white shirt, which had been tailored to span his Nordic proportions, gave proof of other qualities. Even his hands set the stage for the initial impression of ferocity. The elegant hands that splayed across his muscular thighs now. Hands she had felt circle her waist, lift her breasts, tangle in her hair . . .

Her eyes flicked up to his. Through the gloom, his pale eyes gleamed hotly. How those eyes had tortured her over the years! Seeing into her mind, her heart, her very soul . . .

Had she no refuge?

She turned her face to the street. Tears coursed down her cheeks.

She felt, rather than saw, him open his arms to her.

"Liebchen," he beckoned.

Six

"Kommt zu mir," he whispered, and would have pulled her back against him.

But she leaned forward, her forehead to the side of the coach, her shoulders rounding away from him.

He moved back instantly.

She brushed away her tears and sniffled. When she reached for a handkerchief and, of course, found none, he offered her his. She took it and composed herself. Then, very slowly, she turned to face him, sinking into the corner she'd come from.

He was waiting. Farther back in the shadows, he sat, so that she saw only the barest outline of the blond hair, the devastating face. But she saw his hands clearly, and they were once more fanned on his massive thighs. Still. Waiting.

"Thank you for coming," she said into the void.

He waved one hand as if to dismiss the pleasantries.

She fiddled with the handkerchief.

"Naturally, I wanted to talk with you, after last night. I—I was so shocked! So undone I could not think rationally. I was so amazed to see you. So overjoyed to have you there. Oh God! I cannot be coy. I was delirious with joy. Seven years is a terribly long time, and letters are never equal to the flesh and blood man. I enjoyed you there. I could not have wished for a better birthday present. Nor would I have dared to wish for such a thing. Over the years," she fought back tears again, "I have learned not to wish, not to expect *anything* where you are concerned."

She was being brutal and she knew it. She was reaching for destruction. Lashing out at him, the one man, the only man she had ever loved or ever could. But she was on this course, and it was the right one. Amidst all the furor over the murdered man in the park, she had thought this all out very precisely. She knew what she had to do.

"Over the years, I have taken what moments I could, what joys I was offered because I adored you. But last night was so different. For the first time in all the years we have loved each other, you were *here* with me in my home, my country. We were not in some foreign city like Paris, where we could register as man and wife in some small hotel where no one knew us. We were not on a small island like Samos, where we went that summer in '60. We were in my Grandmother Howard's house in London! Don't you see? I—I felt rocked! All those people. All my family. It was heaven to have you there, but—but *torture* that I could not reach out and really touch you, kiss you! Don't you see?" She was giving in to the tears, the choking pain. "Oh, Gus, don't you see, I—?"

"Why don't you touch me now?"

The temptation of a lifetime—ambrosia and nectar for a starving woman. But like Midas, she was near, so near, and now so far.

She shrank farther into the corner. *"Nein! Ich kann dass nicht tun!"* Unconsciously she spoke his language to make her point crystal clear.

He leaned forward, and in the landau's lamplight, those magnificent copen blue eyes bored into hers. *"Warum?"*

"Why? Oh, God, Gus! You know *why!* The minute . . . the second I touch you, I'll be lost."

"Then *I* will touch *you.*"

His hands circled her wrists and his eyes fell to them.

She stopped breathing.

Beneath the black silk, her skin heated as he slowly, painstakingly slid his palms up her arms to her shoulders and her throat, up her jaw to cup her cheekbones. His thumbs rubbed across her cheeks to take away the vestiges of tears. His eyes caressed hers.

"Mein Herz," he murmured.

Her eyes fell closed. *My heart. My heart.*

"Ich verstehe, meine Liebe."

He understood? She didn't. She never had. She was crying again.

"Mirinda," he said now in his perfect, unaccented English. "Look at me, darling."

She did as he requested.

His eyes were moist. "Dry your tears, darling." He lifted her chin and chucked it before he withdrew back into his seat. "Tell me what it is you want."

"I want us to be friends."

"We are. God made us friends in heaven eternities ago."

"I mean just friends. *Only* friends."

He chuckled. "You mean we are not to touch at all, is that it?" He was laughing now.

"I don't find this amusing."

"No, I see you don't. But somehow, it appeals to my sense of humour." He took out another handker-

70

chief from his trouser pocket and wiped his eyes. "What do you mean to do, *Liebchen?* Pretend you are a nun and I am a eunuch?"

Given all the events of last night and tonight, *that* was not funny.

"I mean us to be polite, to enjoy each other when we see each other socially, but—"

"But here in London where everyone knows everyone else who matters, we will be celibate. Yes, I quite understand your point of view."

"But you will debate it with me."

"Natürlich."

"Why? Gus, for God's sake, you are sent by the Kaiser—"

"Really by Bismarck."

"Bismarck, then. You are a special emissary. You are here to negotiate with the government on important diplomatic issues."

"Chinese issues, to begin with."

"Very well, Chinese issues. And you will be involved with the highest strata of society. You'll be giving receptions, dinners, going to balls, and I—

"Will be invited to many of them."

"Precisely."

"Because you come from the same strata, darling."

"Because I am an older, unmarried woman who does not drool over every unattached man in sight."

"Because you are in love with me."

"Because," she glared at him, "many a hostess needs acceptable female company to round out the numbers at her dinner table!"

"And I will be delighted to have you as my dinner partner, darling. My wife is not with me, as usual. Even if she were here, I would be as I always am—

alone and dreaming of you. Yes, I dream. I dream because I have so little else of you. When Bismarck ordered me here, I began to dream more. I *like* my dreams of being your dinner partner here in London, and believe me, I will relish every morsel I am fed and every trifling conversation I encounter as long as I am by your side."

"And I will not!"

"Won't you?"

"No! I cannot afford you, Gus. Not in London. I will make a fool of myself. Wanting to touch you, hold your arm. Wanting to kiss you, embrace you. I can't chance it. I have only to look at you and my body takes fire. I may be fifty, but I still yearn for you. With one errant glance, I could ruin us both! We must not see each other alone. Ever. We *must* be acquaintances. Polite old friends."

Swift as lightning, he had her by the shoulders, lifting her across the seat, across his lap, his lips mere inches from hers.

"You demand from me restraint of the gods. Yet you give me nothing. Do not assume I have not thought of this and worried myself." His fingers dug into her hair. "But I have thirsted for you too long. And life has not been good. I grow older, wiser, lonelier. I need you. I need to be near you. Do not tell me that you will deny me the joy of you, *mein Herz*. If you will not share a bed with me, I did not expect it. I can probably live without that. I have for so many empty years. But do not tell me you will not laugh with me, dance with me, make jokes with me. Life is too short not to take what we can. So . . . we can be friends."

"Can we?" She was lost in his voice, his cologne,

the torment in his eyes.

"On two conditions."

"Which are?"

"Quite different."

"What is the first?"

"Kiss me now. Once." He cocked a wicked brow. "If you do it right, it might satisfy me for another seven years."

She broke out laughing and circled her arms about his massive shoulders to hug him. Their bodies fused together as they both laughed, and she leaned back in his arms, silent.

Once. She would kiss him once.

She smiled into his eyes and he narrowed them at her. Waiting for her.

She raised one hand and ran it across his chiseled, clean-shaven jaw. With the pads of her fingers, she brushed his manly lips. An index finger traced the fencing scar. All five fingers combed into the flaxen thick mass of hair at his temple. At his nape, her hand kneaded the powerful cords of his neck, and slowly, inexorably, she brought his face, inch . . . by inch . . . by inch, down to hers.

Touching and yet not, she placed her mouth on his and felt his ragged breath. *"Mein Herz,"* she whispered, *"Ich liebe dich."* And then she gave him what he wanted, what they both wanted. She kissed him.

She let her lips meet his sweetly. He gathered her closer.

She kissed him deeply. He opened his mouth.

She kissed him sensuously. He groaned.

She kissed him savagely, and he bound her to him so fiercely she thought he would take her into his skin, into his soul.

She lost all sense of time, of reason. Lost all to this never-ending force between them. Before she knew it, she was kissing him a thousand times—his jaw, his cheeks, his eyes, his mouth again.

He was chuckling when he grabbed her wrist again and pressed her into the seat. *"Halt!"*

She stopped immediately, contrite not in the least. "Sorry. I forgot. Just one kiss. Well . . ." she struggled up in his arms and combed shaking fingers through her gnarled hair, "was it worth seven years?"

He narrowed his eyes at her. *"Jawohl."*

"Natürlich," she teased, and he seized her around the waist and clamped her to his chest, his lips against her ear.

"I make this promise—*Liebchen, du bist mein* and I will never hurt you. We will do what we must here in London while we also enjoy our unprecedented proximity. But when it ends, I will exact the other condition."

She nuzzled his throat. "Which is?"

"When I am posted elsewhere, before I go, you will come with me somewhere, anywhere I choose for at least a month or two. Yes, I think *two*. I grow old, darling, and without the sight of you, I die. Promise me that, and I will help you not to ruin us in London."

She pressed her hand to his cheek and cherished his eyes. "Two small favors for the ecstasy of being near you, my love."

He grinned, flashing long white teeth. Then he helped her up and out of his reach. He settled back and crossed his arms.

This pact they had, this joy, this agony would begin now.

But she could live with this. She needed him. His companionship. His counsel. The world was brutal and he was her friend. She sat opposite him and indulged in one thing she'd hardly ever had with him — idle conversation.

"How was your dinner with the Prime Minister?"

"Long, with good cigars and mediocre brandy."

"Do you see Her Majesty soon?"

"Yes, a courtesy call. Since I am not the ambassador from Berlin, I need not present my papers or my person until she has a free minute to receive me. I remain merely her German guest."

"More than that, my love. You are her cousin."

"Distant but related, yes."

The banter lifted her yet made her sad as well. Now that they had their pact, she could not get too far from the vision of the murdered man in the park.

She smoothed her skirts unnecessarily.

"What worries you, *Liebchen?*"

"I am afraid."

"You? I do not believe it. Tell me how this can be."

"Some strange things have happened in the past few months. You know about the baby's body we found in the chimney, but I did not write you all the sordid details."

She swallowed hard and when she opened her mouth, she was suddenly delivering a soliloquy. A soliloquy of horrors about the baby they had found in the chimney, the supreme effort she and Clare had put forth to clear the family name, and finally the tale of the man in the park the previous night.

She explained about Clare's and her financial need to build and rent the townhouses in the Close. How they had let only four and had two more prospective tenants. How the bankers and the builders were demanding their money. And how she didn't blame them, but she didn't have it all just yet. And now, with the death of the Chinese man in the park, she was afraid the four tenants she had would move out. Then where would she and Clare be?

"Oh, Gus. I am positive it will be in the newspapers tomorrow and we shall be besieged with the questions of the world. During the mystery of the baby's death, we weathered the elements quite well. But I am not sure about this time. One murder is extraordinary. Two are uncanny. I cannot afford to lose any commissions, and Clare, though she would deny it, is not yet well from that illness last winter. People talk so furiously about anything and I am afraid they will say things that could not be true."

"Such as?"

"We have created a blight in the neighborhood. Well, you know how that is. Good grief, the East End has as many murders in three months."

"Not quite, my darling." He shifted in his seat and rested one elbow on an armrest, stroking his chin. "Tell me about the Chinese man. How do you know he was Chinese?"

She explained Clare's reasonings.

"I agree. He sounds Chinese. I have been to Japan and Korea, as well as to your British Treaty Ports. The Eastern peoples are very different from each other."

"She says she is confused, though, because he looked well-fed. She thinks he was a gentleman."

He stopped stroking his chin. "Why does she say that?"

Mirinda tried for a smile. "She says he could not be a coolie because his hands were too unscarred, his nails short but clean and manicured."

"Because he did not appear to be a coolie does not mean he was a gentleman, a *literati*."

"Oh, I don't think she meant gentleman in their terms as much as in ours. A man of the upper classes, titled, privileged. A man who was well-fed, not a peasant converted to obtain a bowl of rice, she said."

"I understand many wish to emigrate and why. China is an empire in chaos. Besieged by the Westerners from without, ripped by rebellion and famine and corrupt government from within, many leave the Celestial Middle Kingdom. Though the ones we tend to see most in our Western countries now are the coolies — the poor ones; others would give much to leave. The Empress Dowager is a feared harpy. A witch who often purges the ungrateful or the uncooperative from her midst."

Mirinda shuddered. "Will you go there?"

"No, I do doubt it, my love. Bismarck barely understands colonial politics, and what he knows he knows because I have taught him or I have recommended it. I will not recommend the German Imperial *Reich* seek anything in China except peace. That is why I am here, at least initially. I am one of four special ministers to deal with this. John Newhall for Victoria's government and Charles Beaumont for the French Third Republic, plus Saldahna for the Portuguese in Macao. Together, we will devise a plan to deal with little skirmishes which all too easily become big battles in China.

"Bismarck wants no more wars. Neither do I. The French cannot afford another defeat — God knows, we shoved their faces into the dirt in the Franco-Prussian War five years ago. And the British? Well, they want a way, a peaceful way, to continue to hold as much sway in China as they can."

She admired him and let it show in her eyes. "I know you will be very successful, my love. You always have been."

"Aye, lassie," he imitated a Scotsman's brogue, "I love the way ye admire me so. Now ye d better get on home with ye. Yer sister'll wonder why yer out courtin' after dark."

"No, she won't. She knows."

"You told her?"

"No. I never have to tell Clare things like this. Things of the heart, she knows."

"She knows about Paris and Samos? And Copenhagen?"

"No. Not from my lips. But she can read me. We are twins, do remember. If Robert Murdoch had not been a widower when she met him, she would have done the same as I with you over the years. We Clively sisters love only one man deeply."

He took her hand and pressed a hot, hard kiss into the palm. Then he curled her fingers about it. "Come. I will walk with you to the foot of the drive."

"I will see you soon?"

"My love"—he chucked her under the chin—"you will see me as often as I can arrange it without setting Britain's ears buzzing."

Seven

"Thank you," Clare nodded to the Attenboroughs' butler as she stepped from the vestibule and onto the front steps. When she heard the door latch click closed behind her, she knew she could exhale.

Gad. That had been a mistake. She struck her parasol against the front steps, flicking it open and over her when she reached the sidewalk.

I should have stayed at home and done my weeding. I have accomplished nothing here this afternoon.

Three calls within forty-five minutes had gotten her some information, not all of it what she sought.

At Number 6, Mr Brewster, for example, was at home. Odd for a man, even one in the Commons, to be home at such an hour. His wife did not blink an eyelash, as was good form. However, if the man and his new wife would move because of murder in their midst, Clare could divine nothing.

At Number 8, Mrs Fitzhugh was nervous—but not about the body in the park. Throughout the required quarter hour, the woman kept fidgeting, casting her eyes to the front window and the mantel clock. Clare was obviously intruding, either delaying or menacing some other event. As to whether the Fitzhughs would move, Clare doubted it. Mrs

Fitzhugh was expecting a baby—their fourth, she said—within the year.

The nadir—or the zenith, depending on how Clare saw it—of the three visits so far was her time at Number 10. Fifteen minutes with Mr Attenborough's wife equaled fifteen minutes worth of torture on a Spanish *don's* rack. The woman was either ill or simply had never been trained to carry on a frothy conversation. She was, in fact, quite blunt.

Yes, the police had come yesterday afternoon to talk. Then, as Clare was left to steer their way through the perilous pleasantries of an afternoon call, she was crudely told that the woman wanted all the facts of the murder down to the minutest detail.

Clare declined to repeat all that she'd seen and deduced. Aside from the fact that it was simply none of Mrs Attenborough's business, she did not want to appear as though she were encouraging speculation. Of course, the climax came the minute Clare discovered the Attenboroughs would not move because of publicity.

"My husband says he is here until he acquires enough money to buy a house equal to what Scarborough House once was before you and your sister cut it in two. Yes, he likes the Close very much, Lady Murdoch. He says he intends to make Attenborough a name to remember," the pug-faced woman had explained, "just as the name Clively once was."

Soon after, her teeth grinding to nubs, Clare excused herself.

She had only one more call to make and then she

could remove this infernal corset, perhaps burn it, and have a cup of tea. Then, she would reward herself and do her weeding.

Clare passed Mirinda's and then her own front door as she made her way to Number 20. This would be the most delightful of the visits. This she had saved for last.

She made her way up the six steps, so similar to the other facades, and smiled to herself. All the townhouses in the circle looked alike. She and Mirinda and the architects had planned it that way for uniformity, consistency, and serenity.

She herself had insisted on the serenity. An avid artist, when the mood took her, she had an eye for such things and did not want the Close cluttered with any more foolish Victorian "muscularity" or "gewgaws" than was necessary.

As for uniformity, only the details of the houses differed. The style and the paint on the trim. The shade of the brick. The shape of the turrets that rose from the second stories for one more elevation.

Yes, she liked Clively Close very much.

The houses and the thought of the person she was about to call upon made her lips curl in a smile as Lee Davenport's butler answered her knock.

"Good afternoon, milady." The Englishman seemed out of breath and smiled tremulously at Clare as he allowed her to enter the ivory-tiled hall.

"Good afternoon, Williams. I have come to call on Mrs Davenport. I realize I came only last week, but I did hope she might be at home to me today."

"I will inquire, milady," he said, and she noticed that he was not as buoyant as last week. "Come with me, madam."

She followed him into the drawing room to the right of the foyer, and he left her there to admire the decor. Like last week, she reveled in it. At base an English drawing room, this had all the elements decreed by society. The front window swathed in yards of drapery. One massive fireplace, quite blank in the June afternoon. Two matching settees, facing each other at right angles to the fireplace. Chairs here and there, of all sizes and shapes, confirmed the fact that the widowed Mrs Davenport intended to entertain in a grand manner in her new residence in London, England.

But there the normal ended and the delight began.

The walls were painted daisy-yellow and trimmed in glowing white. Above the mantel stood a Chinese painting of the Sung school. An ethereal green landscape of willows and flowering cherry trees, a waterfall, and one Buddhist pagoda nestled into a mountainside upon the four-paneled canvas. A T'ang sculpture of a gold horse with jade saddle and green-clad rider sat upon a carved credenza of teak. The Chippendale settees, the Western interpretation of the Chinese form, were enhanced by the forest-green brocade upholstery and in dark contrast to the thick pile of the sea-blue wool Chinese rug. The chairs, it was true, were a symphony of Western styles made all the more harmonious by the variegated shades of greens and blues and purples. Throughout, on this lacquered table or that rosewood one, a thousand expressions of the Chinese art of the ages graced the room.

So pleasing to the eye, this room would enchant many who visited and then went home to a murky mix of mauves and purples and blood-reds. Indeed, if Clare were ever forced to part with the family furniture that had graced Scarborough House for centuries, she would replace it all in a moment and create this.

Out in the hallway, someone whispered frantically and someone else replied. Their tone said they were arguing. A third person, a woman, stopped the debate. Another woman shushed the entire group. Calm prevailed, punctuated only by numerous footsteps.

But when the drawing room doors swung inward, there stood Lee Davenport with a smile on her face. Behind her, hobbling up the stairs on teetering Manchu slippers, a maid at her side, was one very pregnant woman.

Because the woman was almost at the top of the flight, Clare caught only a glimpse of her feet. Tiny, gnarled little appendages in the absurdly elevated shoes, combined to render a woman almost utterly dependent on her servants—and her husband.

But her slippers were treacherous and the stairs steep. She stumbled, grasping the railing, and Williams, who had followed the woman and the maid, reached out to break her fall.

What a mistake! The woman shrank from Williams, her eyes wide with fright at his hands upon her arms. In bell-like tones, she registered a pointed complaint with the maid. The English servant only stared and shrugged at her Chinese language, then helped the woman up.

But in those few moments, Clare glimpsed the Chinese woman's profile and almost gasped aloud.

She was exquisite, finely dressed in red silk pyjamas, finely coiffed with long hair ornaments, finely boned, and oddly, sans the usual cosmetics of powder and vermilion lip rouge.

"Lady Clare!" Lee Davenport, who had spun around to view the incident, turned back to her guest with an apologetic but terrified smile. "She is well. My cousin, who visits me, insists on wearing traditional Chinese garb. Do not be concerned. She will soon learn those Manchu slippers are not meant for Western houses."

Clare swung her eyes to Lee and lost all sense of reason. In its place rose a violent declaration from the very air around her: *I am not welcome here today.*

Still, she and Lee smiled broadly at each other and went about the initial polite bits of banter.

But all the while, Clare was wondering *why* she had such an insight. For certainly, insight it was, though in truth, there was nothing in Lee's behavior that said Clare was not appreciated.

Lee, tall as her British father and raven-haired as her half-Chinese, half-British mother, nodded and ushered Clare to two facing chairs in a small grouping near the front bay window. Perched on the edge of her seat as was customary for a courtesy call, Clare explained why she was there.

"My dear Mrs Davenport—"

"I thought last week we had agreed to be less formal, and you were to call me what you called me when I was a child." Lee's black eyes twinkled with kindness.

"Then, if that is true, my dear Lee, you must leave off with addressing me as Lady Clare."

"I am sorry," she blushed, dropping her gaze to her hands. "The rituals of a lifetime die hard. I shall always remember the first day I saw you. My father introduced you to my mother and I watched behind the garden trellis. You were *Lady Clare* to her. *A grand lady,* she said to me often. She loved you so, Clare. You were the only English lady who ever accepted her as Mrs Ashton. The only English lady who received her in your parlour. She never forgot that and neither have I."

"Thank you, my dear. I loved your mother very much. She was very good to me and did me great honour by receiving me. I am very much in her debt, you know. I would not have had the wonders of the Chinese universe opened to me if it were not for the teachings of your mother. And when my husband died so suddenly," Clare caught her voice to speak of the very thing she dared not remember with any detail, "your mother was my bulwark. My strength."

Lee nodded, her heart-shaped face passive, her liquid black eyes commiserating with the woman before her. "I knew I could come to you for advice when I first decided to move here and claim my husband's estate. It seems our lives—my mother's and mine and yours—move in a circle. You helped my mother. She helped you. You help me, yet again. I hope someday I might assist you once more and complete another cycle, Clare."

"Is that not the essence of the Chinese universe, Lee? The completion of cycles? I find myself at the end of one and beginning another even now."

Clare surprised herself with that statement. *Was it true?* Before she had a full answer, she let herself move on, discovering as she spoke her own subterranean thoughts.

"I find myself remembering more clearly today things from twenty years ago." *Love. Death. Grief.* "I discover myself creating things which recall my past." *Which fix it and quantify it.* "The gazebo I told you about last week . . . even its gardens remind me of the wonderful two years I had in China, especially Shanghai."

"I wanted to see it Saturday evening," Lee said.

"Yes, but the early evening rain drenched everything. I was very disturbed we had to move the event inside. But why not come one afternoon for tea, and we will sit there and you may comment on my attempt at a Chinese garden."

"I would be delighted to come." Lee's eyes clouded with concern and flicked away a moment before she caught herself. "I miss Shanghai, and your pagoda and garden may do much for my melancholy."

"I know, my dear. I myself have spent many years learning to live without my husband." *I may just be beginning. Just beginning? After twenty years? Where did that thought spring from?* The training of a lifetime made her shake herself and press on with this conversation. "Forgive me, Lee, for being so brash, but . . . well, your parents and my husband and I were fast friends."

"Oh, Clare, please do not apologize. I welcome the opportunity to talk about my husband with someone. He was—" she was trying so valiantly not to cry. "He was a wonderful man. Brave and kind."

"Yes," Clare whispered. Then she reached across the space dividing them and covered Lee's delicate hands to stop her from wringing them white. "When one loves completely, it is heartrending to come to terms with the finality of the relationship."

"He suffered because of our marriage," Lee continued. "He said he didn't, but I knew. The British Army does not favour men who marry colonial natives or even half-castes. They ignore them. We were not invited to dine with the customs officials nor the special emissaries Britain sent to Shanghai. My husband was kept in that post for too long, not promoted as he should have been. Willard worked very hard at the garrison. His men adored him and followed him anywhere, even beyond the Settlement walls. But it meant little compared to the fact that General Willard Gooding Davenport had married a Chinese woman."

Clare knew she spoke the truth. Clare had seen it firsthand. In Africa, India, and China. The British, God Save the Queen, went out to trade with the world and found themselves controlling it. Governing it, educating it, changing it, transforming it. And all the while acquiring an innate *hauteur* that became none of them and conflicted with whatever beneficial aspects of Western culture they sought to gift others. Racial discrimination was one of those examples of *hauteur* that preserved the hegemony of the British Empire while it ate at its power from within.

"I know the day will come when the Western world values China and its culture."

"But that day, dear Clare, is not today. In Shanghai, I moved through British society with Willard more easily than my mother had with my father. I am only one-quarter Chinese and can pass as a white woman if one does not look too closely at my eyes. Some thought I looked Irish. Imagine! But those who mattered knew who I was. The daughter of another British general posted to the Settlement and *his* half-Chinese wife."

"Your mother suffered, yes. But she knew what she was doing when she married your father. So did your father. She told me one afternoon as we sat in her garden. She was instructing me in calligraphy. An odd thing for even a Chinese woman to know in those days. But she was teaching me how to write *harmony* and I was not applying myself. She told me how Chinese society constantly strived for harmony but it was merely a vision for many, never a reality. That was during the Taiping Rebellion. The rebel forces made a march for Shanghai's gates. Her husband and mine worked night and day to fortify the Settlement's defenses. She said harmony had eluded her life and only with her husband in the confines of their home did she find any."

"And yet she knew about English culture and had more Western learning than many an English lady."

"Yes," Clare mused. "As the daughter of a Hong Kong *taipan* and his Cantonese wife, she was extraordinary in many ways."

"My mother spoke four languages. Did you know that? She used to laugh when the Western officers would come to my father's house to meet and a few of them would speak in their own tongues to be secretive—and afterward she could repeat their conversations for my father word for word. The men always thought my father was shrewd. He never told them his secret was his wife!"

"Your grandmother, your mother, and you lived

in difficult times, under difficult circumstances. And now you are here in England to begin a new adventure. A different kind."

"Yes, and it is not without its perils. What will a rich, landed, partly Chinese widow do with all that money?" Her eyes roamed the room. "Clare, I cannot imagine it. Willard would have been absolutely astounded to learn he was the sole heir to his grandfather's estate. Willard purchased his commission in his regiment because he thought there was no hope of him ever having any inheritance. They looked down on him even for that, because he was the son of an English tea trader and not a lord's third or fourth son." She sighed. "I don't know if I shall stay here too long, Clare. Unless I am allowed to breathe easily about my status, I may simply return to Shanghai after the legalities are finalized."

"I understand, my dear. But times are still troublesome in China."

"Yes, the rebellions are small and furtive. Shanghai is still a hotbed of unrest, with factory riots and hatred of the Westerners, especially the missionaries. The suffering among the common man is awful. Many work from dawn to dusk and still starve. The Imperial Government increases taxes constantly, trying to modernize and make China more like the West. But the taxes would not be so awful if the *literati,* the government officials, did not exact their squeeze. The oppression forces many to the Treaty Ports for work or on to a ship out to some other country."

This point about Chinese émigrés suddenly troubled Clare as it never had before. Until this moment, Clare had made no connection between the murdered man in the park being Chinese and the fact that Lee was partially so. But now she did.

"Would you return, Lee? Shanghai is a dangerous place to live, especially for a woman who is partly English."

"My dear Clare, any place is a dangerous place to live." Her eyes told Clare she knew where her mind led.

"The police have been here, then."

"And questioned me for over two hours. Then they moved on to question my staff."

Clare wondered what they had asked but knew she could not question Lee, lest she sound rude.

"But I told them I did not know any Chinese men here in London. The man was Chinese but my staff is not. None of them."

Yes, Clare knew that Lee's entire staff was very English, chosen only recently by Lee upon Clare's advice.

Yet, what of the woman climbing the stairs?

She was about to give birth. Where, then, was her husband? Clare wondered if she had one. But, if she did not, how had she arrived safely in England and why?

Unable to ask, Clare chose another route.

"It was terrible to find him in such a condition. Did they tell you I found him? Yes. Awful sight. No idea how or why someone would do such a thing. It is so barbaric."

Lee raised both black brows and anger lit her eyes. "Barbaric, yes. The very word the Chinese use to denote the Westerner."

"Yes." Quite. Clare fought for some other line of reasoning. Contrary to her usual politeness, Lee did not assist her. The silence throbbed between them, and finally, Clare put them both out of their misery.

"Whoever he was, he did not deserve that."

"No. His ancestors will not receive him very easily. He was so deformed by his attacker."

Lee referred to the Confucian veneration of the body and the belief that it should pass intact to the grave. This man's body would not.

Clare suddenly recalled Robert's description of one Chinese criminal he had seen in the streets. When he came upon him, the man was dead. His queue had been threaded through a hole at the top of a crosslike rack to keep the body in position while a rope around his neck had been slowly twisted until strangulation occurred. Greater offenses merited greater punishments—most of them mutilations, destructions of the body. For petty thievery, a relatively minor offense, a criminal's body was marred very little. He was flogged, albeit publicly. For theft of money, a criminal could die by strangulation. The idea was that he would be returned to his ancestors with some semblance of his body's sanctity.

Only for murder or high treason against the person of the emperor—the ultimate crimes—was the ultimate punishment exacted. Decapitation. Again, done publicly. To insure that the criminal did not go to his ancestors at all. To serve as a disgrace and a warning to others tempted to commit the same crime.

But the man in the park had been denied physical sanctity and dignity in a Chinese and a Western sense. Why?

"Why do you suppose the perpetrator did that to him, Lee?"

Lee shrugged. "To disgrace him, I suppose."

Clare would not let it go. "There seem to be so many punishments in China coded to the exact crime." Was there some code whose breach was punished by castration? Clare had never heard of one. But she had to find out if Lee knew.

So she asked.

Lee shifted visibly in her chair. "Please, Clare. Do not talk about it." She put a hand to her mouth as if she were about to become ill.

"Oh, I am sorry, Lee. I did not mean to distress you."

But I have. And now I must know why.

"I shall leave you, my dear Lee. Thank you for receiving me. I enjoyed our little chat. Do come to tea . . . shall we say Thursday?"

"Thursday is wonderful."

"I look forward to it."

Lee rose and extended a hand toward the door. "I will see you out."

"Yes, Williams must be very busy with your cousin." Then, before Lee had a chance to cover her confusion, Clare added, "Do bring her to tea, too."

"Oh—oh, I am afraid she does not know the Western traditions of teatime, Clare. She would feel out of place. And she speaks no English. I—"

Clare waved a hand. "My dear, you know I will try to make her comfortable. Do all in my power to welcome her. I do speak a little Mandarin."

Lee was left groping. "She is from Canton."

Cantonese? Clare replayed the sounds of the

92

woman's reprimand in her brain. That was no Cantonese she spoke. No, it was Mandarin, the dialect Clare knew.

Lee was continuing, covering. "She visits me for a few months."

"Until the birth of her baby, I would venture."

"Yes . . . the birth of her baby." Lee forced her lips into a smile. "I do not know if Yi-an will be able to come with me. She cannot walk very easily nor for very long distances."

"Yes. I saw. She has bound feet." Clare was smiling as she rifled through her memory of Lee's family, trying to recall exactly who was still so stolidly Chinese to bind a baby girl's feet and cripple her for life. "Odd. I don't remember any one of your family who believed in the beauty of the 'lily feet.' "

"She is a distant cousin. From my grandmother's family. They observe the old traditions. She would not have made a good marriage without the foot binding."

"Ahh, yes. And she is lovely. So of course, she would marry well. Is her husband here in England also?"

"No. He is dead."

At this, Clare held her breath and examined Lee's troubled eyes. "I am so sorry to hear that. She comes to England only to be widowed."

"No. Her husband died before she left Shanghai."

The speed with which Lee said it left no doubt in Clare's mind that she spoke the truth. Yi-an's lack of makeup and coiffure, with hair parted down the middle, also denoted her status as widow. So. The man in the park truly was not the cousin's husband.

"She must be very frightened, then, to be alone

93

in a new country on the eve of the birth of her baby."

"Yes, very much so." Obviously grateful to discuss some other aspect of her cousin, Lee went on. "Her trip was long and arduous. She dislikes ships. This is her first child and she is very delicate."

"She is very far along, I would assume from what I saw. Well, my dear, when it is her time, if you have any trouble, do come to me. I will recommend a good doctor."

"Oh, no! She would never use a *doctor!*"

"She has an aversion to Western medicine, does she?"

So many Chinese distrusted the Westerners' science. Even in the Treaty Ports, they preferred their ancient remedies of herbs and spices, acupuncture and massage, even necromancers predictions, to alleviate their bodily ills.

"No. I will deliver this baby myself. She has a long-standing rule in her family. No man except her husband may ever touch her."

"But, my dear, you have no practice in delivering babies, do you? It is not an easy task and she—"

"She will need no one but me." Lee was firm, and not only once again angry but now doubly anxious as well.

"Yes, of course," Clare murmured. "If such is the case, however, my sister and I do have a close friend who is a woman *and* a doctor. Her name is Blackwell. Dr Elizabeth Blackwell. She has specialized in the treatment of women here in London. So if you do need help, Lee, please . . . I hope you will call on us."

"Yes, certainly." Lee bit her lip.

Clare smiled, recognizing anguish when she saw it. "Good day, my dear Lee." She resisted the urge to let her eyes travel up the stairs as she accepted her parasol from Lee's shaking hands. "Until Thursday."

Eight

She awoke with a start.

The room was empty. Silent. Dark.

She struggled up on one elbow and reached for her flannel-lined silk bed jacket lying across the boudoir chair.

She would not sleep now. The image had been too vivid. Too disturbing.

She had to get up and capture it now lest it disappear.

She stuck her feet into her bed slippers and padded across her bedroom to her sitting room. Grabbing up her sketch pad and two soft graphite pencils, she turned up the gas on the wall sconces and settled into her favorite place, her white eyelet chaise lounge.

The comfort soothed her muddled mind, surrounding her troubled senses and setting the sixth one free.

The feeling was upon her. She knew it. She had only to close her eyes and let it come . . . come.

Her hand flew across the paper. The pencils did not suit. One was too dull. The other broke. In a fit, she dashed them to the floor. She scooped up the stick of charcoal from her escritoire and let her hand do what it willed. Purposely, she allowed the dream to speak through her hands.

With quick strokes and subtle shadings, she formed a face. A delicate face. Without makeup, as widows were supposed to be. But with dark hair, parted in the middle, and dangling hair ornaments atop two large curling buns, one over each ear. Earrings, long and full of gemstones. Finely shaped, winged brows over sad eyes. Tearing eyes. Large, almond-shaped, incomparable crying eyes. Around her neck a scarf. A long scarf.

Clare's hand paused, falling.

There was no more to the image. No more to the vision.

Clare sat staring at it for a very long time before she acknowledged that the terror that had awakened her was this one. Yi-an was crying because she was dying. Dying because the scarf was strangling her. *Her.*

The scarf, which by its length and by its fringe, if not by its color, was really Clare's rendering of the one that belonged to the man in the park . . .

"The newspapers say little about the murder this morning, Clare." Mirinda sailed in at half nine, dressed to her hat, and threw down yesterday's and today's newspapers beside Clare on her dining room table. "I am glad of it. I don't think I could have borne more."

Clare eyed her sister. Odd for Mirinda not to love a challenge. But then again, not so odd, considering what must be running through her mind the past few days.

Clare put down her cup and nodded. "I am sur-

97

prised Ann Billings Wentworth did not pester you more than she did yesterday."

"She was very sweet about it, really. I simply recounted what we knew, which was exactly what the police know — and the *Times* and all of London, know." Mirinda was tugging on her gloves, headed for some appointment. "She was sad she had not gotten the exclusive story. But what could I do? This case is not like the other. We don't know things others don't."

Clare stared at her.

Mirinda opened her mouth to bid her sister goodbye and then promptly clamped it shut. *Oh, God.* She knew that look.

She took a seat and removed her gloves.

"What do we know," she asked on a thread, "that others do not?"

Clare tilted her head to one side and began to speak.

Mirinda leaned across the table and examined her twin's features. Clare was tight, drawn, weary-looking this morning.

"Are you ill again? You did not sleep well, did you? How is your chest? Tight? You need to be out in the sun more. Yes, yes, I know you worked in the gardens yesterday. I saw you from my studio window. But you must take better care of yourself. You—"

"Indy."

"Tell me."

"No, I am not ill again. No, I did not sleep well. Yes, my chest is clear, dear. I worked in the garden in the late afternoon sun and felt wonderful afterward. I am recovering, Indy. Do not fret over that."

"But there is some other matter I should fret over."

Clare nodded.

Mirinda's eyes grew round. "What is it? What's happened?"

"I told you last night before you went out to the Maccarrans' dinner party that I had made my calls and discovered little of use. That was not quite true."

"But—"

"I did not want you burdened with more than was necessary. Gus was at the Maccarrans', wasn't he?"

"Yes. He received a last-minute invitation yesterday morning. Leslie Maccarran is Under Secretary and it was only good form for Gus to be included."

"That's what I surmised. I know what a trying time this is for you, Indy. I kept my thoughts to myself because I needed to sort them out myself. What you must know is that my visit to Lee Davenport left me with more questions than the one I walked in with. And I have spent most of the night searching for answers."

Indy removed her hat and jabbed the long pin into the straw with a vicious dig. "Hats. Hate the things." She combed escaping tendrils of hair back from her temples.

"Tea?" Clare asked absently.

"No."

"Lee Davenport has recently acquired a houseguest. The houseguest arrived since last week when I visited. The guest and any discussion of her sends Lee into a whirlwind of anxiety and anguish."

Indy snorted. "Nothing new. I daresay we've had

a few guests we wished to throw out with the morning's swill."

"Hmm. Not like this one. This one is young, lovely, and a widow. She will deliver a baby any day, speaks Cantonese which is really Mandarin, and cannot allow a man—*any* man to touch her. Lee declares the woman is her cousin, yet her feet are bound, and for over four decades the *taipan* Derwenter family has forbidden anyone to bind their female children'ss' feet."

Mirinda chuckled and crossed her arms. "Now *I* have more questions than what I walked in with!"

"I think they know the man in the park."

"Why?"

Clare lifted her shoulders. "A feeling."

"One of your *voyants?*"

"Yes, but stronger."

"How strong?"

"I drew a sketch."

"Of the feeling."

"Precisely."

"My God. You have never done that before. Why? Why do you do it now? Before your feelings have always been . . ." Mirinda waved a hand, ever adverse to truly defining it for fear it might disappear.

"Nothing more than impressions. Insights."

Indy nodded. "A knowledge of human behavior."

"I wondered about that myself—why I would draw this time, that is. I think I know more facts than many—and they fit, but others do not. I—I don't know it all and I—" She inhaled and her whole body seemed suffused with some ethereal joy. She slid her hand to Mirinda's and squeezed it in

100

delight. "And I want to!" Her voice dropped to a hush. "I spent the evening going through my memorabilia from China. The rosewood trunk in my dressing room."

She was up and out of the chair now, beginning to pace.

"I haven't had the courage to look in that trunk since years ago when I came upon the pearl earrings Robert gave me the day before he died. But I opened the trunk last night and, Mirinda"—she swirled about to face her sister, a winning smile on her lips—"I took out everything. Everything!

"The silk robes from Süchow. The blue and white Ming porcelains. The sandalwood fans. Ivory combs. Good God! All of those wonderful treasures locked away! Why do we do such things?"

Mirinda knew the answer as well as Clare. Love does many things to a person, sometimes affirming one emotion and robbing another.

Clare was raking her light brown hair, clutching her upper arms and pacing, pacing.

"I set them around me like scenery from my past. And ooh, the memories returned like a flood. Fast and furious and devastating!"

Mirinda was out of her chair now, coming toward Clare. "My dear, you know what happens when you remember. I don't think your health—"

"No!" Clare thrust up a hand. "No, Indy. Hear me out. My health is improving and will continue to do so. Especially now. Now that I have left behind remorse and chosen to value the other elements of my life with Robert. How instructive, how enlightening, how exhilarating my life was. And I remembered it all.

"I remembered being received by the richest merchant in Hong Kong, the much-feared Gregory Derwenter, the great *taipan,* and his Chinese wife, Lotus. I remembered her perfect English and her joy when she told me about her love for her Western husband. I remembered meeting her second daughter a year later in Shanghai.

"The daughter had married a British Army officer, General Ashton, and Robert took me to introduce me because he thought the lady needed a friend. She did. She was a general's wife but not admitted to good British society. She spoke four languages, which she had learned in her home in Hong Kong from the foreign white devils. But she spoke three Chinese dialects and taught me Mandarin, the Chinese of the Imperial Court. She had children, lovely children, and the loveliest was the only daughter Li. A shy child, snubbed like her siblings by British and Chinese, but intelligent—and honest."

Clare fixed Mirinda with a blank stare. "The woman I talked with yesterday was honest with me about a few facts. She lied about so much more."

"She claims, then, she does not know the man in the park?"

Clare nodded. "Yet his condition, the way he was murdered, gives her great grief. More than someone who is not acquainted with a victim. Yes, Lee knows who he is. And somehow he is connected to the cousin. The cousin of the delicate beauty and condition. The comely cousin who seems to have appeared alone from nowhere and yet is rich enough to wear the finest silk, Manchu heels, and jewelry. A rich cousin who speaks Mandarin. Who speaks in haughty ones to the staff and who merits assistance from them."

"Clare, what are you saying?"

"I am saying the lady has appeared on Lee Davenport's doorstep rather unexpectedly. How did she come? She would not, could not, in her condition, travel alone. I venture to say she came escorted by one man, our man in the park. And now, Lee is terrified the police will return."

"Why should they if they have not the cultural background to deduce what you have deduced, my dear?"

"Precisely." Clare leveled sad eyes at her twin, "I spoke with Ian this morning."

"And?"

"Lee Davenport told them about a new female guest in her house. She said the lady was her cousin."

"Exactly what she told you."

"Yes. But the Dawes brothers didn't ask anything else about the cousin."

"Should they?"

"Oh, but of course! They should ask how she came and with whom?"

"I see." Mirinda sank down in her chair.

"I told Ian about her. He doubts they will return to question any of us in the Close, however."

"Oh, why is that?"

"Without any clues to lead them to a suspect, the Yard begins to doubt a culprit can be found. They will probably put it down to a tussle among immigrants. A squabble over trinkets or stolen goods."

"Even though Clively Close is not the East End docks?!" Mirinda sniffed. "An unsolved murder in our midst. Not a pretty idea, I'll say. Suppose the murderer decides to try it again? How happy will the detectives at the Yard be then?"

Clare smiled.

No, Mirinda realized. Clare *grinned*.

"What are you planning?"

"A little shopping."

"Shopping?"

"Well, you see, it occurs to me that Robin and Sarah Mattingly's wedding day approaches in three weeks and we have not yet sent them wedding gifts. And so I thought that if I—"

It was Mirinda's turn to put up a palm. "Wait a minute, Clare. *You* are going *shopping*. For a wedding present. Why are you going shopping for a wedding present when we were just now discussing how the Yard had turned up no clues in the matter of a murder?"

"Well, you see, my dear, that's because the men at the Yard don't go shopping. And they should."

"They should," Indy muttered, and flapped her hands at her sides. "Why, Clare?"

"Because to find the right information one has to look in the right places, and the Close is not the right place."

"No?"

"Absolutely not. When one goes shopping for clues, one goes to the places a few may reside."

"Such as?"

"Such as, in this case, the places one can find a few experts who might tell more tales than Lee Davenport is willing to part with."

"Who might that be? The only people I have met who seem to understand the Orient are you and

Gus!" Mirinda froze, realizing all too late she'd given away a clue only Clare would match to any *voyant* she might have had about the Prince Hesse-bogen and her sister.

She stared at Clare, whose face was blank. Her twin would ignore this outburst. Take it for its factual value and keep its knowledge in her heart. Very well, pertinence was the order of the day.

Mirinda's mind spun back to the threads of their discourse. Who else would know about the Orient? She smiled. "Of course. Oriental art dealers!"

"Oriental importers. They pick up as much information and gossip in their trade as a good maid. I did think I would start with the better dealers. The Eastern Import Company in Piccadilly. And the Ballantine Emporium in Jermyn Street. I could also invite Lord Reginald Albert's youngest son to luncheon. He works at Christie's, you remember, and he is such a nice young man. Fenton or Denton or perhaps Benton's his name. Gad, do you think I'm becoming like Cousin Alice, confusing names? I do hope not. Anyway, Lord Albert's son knows quite a bit about Orientalia and we can have a nice little chat about it all. Then, if he can impart nothing, perhaps the pawn shops are in order."

Mirinda was wide-eyed with horrified amusement. "A pawn shop. *You* are going to a *pawn* shop? How will you know what you seek?"

"Oh, my dear, I have a very definite idea of what I seek. Fu dogs."

"Pardon me?"

"Fu dogs. Two of them. I have only one. I found it in the truck last night. I have no idea what could have happened to its mate. But I do know I need two. One never gives one fu dog, you see. Bad form. Bad luck, actually. Fu dogs are given to newly married couples for good luck, long life, and many children. They are not quite the most appropriate present for Robin and Sarah, because neither of them expects children at such a late age. But, of course, no one need know to whom the two dogs will go. If they believe it's for Julia's marriage to Dominik Swinford, the Earl of Berwick, then it isn't my fault."

"And it gives you a legitimate, well-publicized excuse to tour shops night and day, because the Clively-Swinford wedding in ten days is the major social event of the summer."

"Exactly. And no one need know I've already sent Julia and Dominik their gift."

Clare sat back with a satisfied smirk.

Perhaps too satisfied? Could Clare transform a shopping expedition into a fact-finding tour? Mirinda had seen her sister maneuver many a disastrous social situation to her ends. What harm could a search for a wedding present do? None, if one asked the right questions and perceived all the right answers, given or omitted. And if anyone perceived correct form and its lack, it was Clare.

And though Mirinda admitted to herself she was appalled at Clare's nerve, she was more delighted with the first aggressiveness and *élan* she'd seen from her sister in two decades.

"You will be discreet with these shopkeepers and Fenton whatever-his-name-is, won't you? Not tell them all you suspect? God knows, I don't want *you* hurt in a park."

"Mirinda, dear, what harm could there be in

106

shopping?"

"What harm, indeed," she muttered. "When do you begin?"

"Tomorrow. Today I go to tea and the Assyrian exhibit at The Henworth with John Newhall."

"Is that so?" Mirinda, who had started to pin on her hat, paused. For the first time in months, Clare's gray eyes snapped with the intelligence and humour that endeared her to her family and friends. Her cheeks were flushed a delicate pink and her heart-shaped mouth curved in a smile Mirinda could only describe as "secretive."

What had occasioned this? John Newhall?

No answers in Clare's clothing. Her dimity dress of peach and green checks was one of the newer members of Clare's extensive wardrobe. Mirinda sniffed, looking down at her own stiffly proper navy faille skirt and white high-necked blouse. Twins, and they had little in common, except intelligence, good humour, and love for each other and family.

She assayed her sister. Could there be that much change in only two or three days? Impossible! Yet, in that new dress, Clare looked decidedly different. The weight she had lost during her last illness was now not as gaunt on her as it was slenderizing. And the effect accentuated her voluptuous figure. Firm, high breasts and a twenty-seven-inch waist on a fifty-year-old woman. Really! It was too exasperating for words! Unless . . .

"Since when do you take tea with a man?"

"Since he asked me Saturday evening."

"You did not tell me."

"*When* could I have done it?"

"Hmmm, true." She drew on her lace gloves. "Since we speak of invitations, we are invited to Gus's this Saturday for dinner. The invitation arrived early this morning with his assistant, Baron von Macht. Colette told me you were still asleep. I hope you don't mind that I replied for us both."

"I don't mind. But tell me, dear, what did we say?"

Last night's dinner was one thing, an unexpected thing, an event Clare was positive Indy could weather without disgrace. But to make such meetings a planned event? Clare pondered.

Mirinda's hazel eyes met hers. They were free of anguish, full of reassurance. "We said we would be happy to accept."

Clare grinned. "I hoped we'd be happy."

Mirinda arched both brows in glee. So . . . both of them had "man" secrets, did they? "We are decidedly happy, indeed."

Nine

His eyes were gray, not brown. His hair was finely wrought silver and straight, not rich mahogany and thick as chocolate cream. But he had a pleasant smile and good manners and a ready quip.

Clare could appreciate him.

She really could. She took another bite of her strawberry tart and smiled and nodded. He was imparting the workings of his day and she was not listening.

Instead, she was finding new things to like about him. After all, she and he had been acquaintances, even friends, one might say, for over three decades, so that she knew the ordinary things.

His family were from Kent. Had been since William of Normandy conquered the isle. Over the centuries, the exalted position of Premier Barony of England conveyed instant recognition of who they were if no concomitant fortune to polish its brilliance.

He had done what was required. He'd gone to Oxford, not performing terribly well, but as a younger, untitled, unmoneyed son, he knew he had to work for a living. He decided he would enter the foreign service. His father, the twenty-first Baron Newhall, obliging papa that he was, had done his duty by the boy and secured a place for him as a private secretary to a Whitehall auditor. The job hadn't paid much, but he had learned quite a bit. The next time a more comely position was vacated, he asked the Baron, his father, to speak to one of his friends in his club to see if John might be considered for a post abroad.

"Calcutta. The Punjab. The Treaty Ports. Back to Calcutta. Burma. My God, Clare. I could write a book!"

"Not a bad idea, John. What better way to tell others you know your subject? So many who would proclaim policy for the colonial territories know nothing of the indigenous cultures. If explorers like Richard Burton find an audience, imagine what a man with your background could inspire."

"Every man needs an Isabel to his Burton." Referring to the famous explorer Richard and his pushy wife, John lifted both brows with bright hope dancing in his gray eyes.

A bulwark, a defender, a mentor, a wife. Before Clare could consider the idea fully, she was covering her indecision with light but self-critical evasion. "The lady is quite rabid, from what I understand. I was brought up with too much attention to propriety, John. If I am avid over an issue, I was taught to hide it. *Well.*"

He put down his teacup and became more circumspect. "I hope that does not bode ill for me."

"It needn't."

"Good. I have waited too long . . ." He drifted off, perplexed.

She knew he was unable to continue on that course. It was too soon in this new relationship he

110

cultivated with her to proclaim ultimate desires more than once and in anything but a congenial fashion. Nor would she have wanted him to venture into the wilds of affectionate declarations so soon.

She needed time. Not so much to become accustomed to him, but to become accustomed to her own unique interests in . . . well, as Aunt Pru had put it, in a dalliance.

"It is difficult," he began again, his manicured fingers rimming the gilt-edged saucer. "I have spent my years devoting myself to my work and I have not thought of meeting a lady for tea or an afternoon at a museum in so very long. I loved my wife, you know. She married me knowing I had little coming to me and that I had to make my way in the Foreign Office or not at all. She was a tolerant woman."

"And she loved you dearly." Clare remembered the sweet little wren who had been his wife. "She feared for you in Calcutta. The riots in '60 were so devastating."

"Some of my posts were so strife-torn I could not take her with me. Oh, I wanted to, but her health deterred that. When I was abroad, I even hated to write to her and tell her exactly how bad it really was. She was not as strong as you. I could not bear to have her worry. But irony of ironies, in the end, it was not worry over me—or some foreign disease—that killed her, but typhoid here at home."

Clare wished they were alone and not in this very proper, very populated tearoom. She wanted so badly to put her hand on his but she couldn't.

"She would be very proud of you today, John."

"Yes. I think she would." He raised his eyes to

Clare's and smiled weakly. "She would find justification in all the years of hard work, wouldn't she?" He laughed, a deep, hearty sound that brought a smile to Clare's lips. "Vindication, I'd say! For all the years she believed in me and I despaired!"

"This special diplomatic group you form with Saldahna, Beaumont, and the Prince Hessebogen is a very important one. And all of you have specific knowledge of the East. It was bound to happen that those who have lived there would rise to a level to decide what occurs there."

"Yes. It has taken too long, though, I fear. Particularly for China. She wastes away from within and without. We cannot bolster her government against her own indifference. The Throne is too corrupt, the government officials, too. They blame it on the Western devils, but we have not done it single-handedly. The Chinese Dragon now feeds upon herself. We four cannot stop her. We can only delay the day she dies."

Discussing international politics was not the norm for a lady and gentleman at tea. A lady and gentleman who were not married to each other were supposed to keep to the social rigours. Yet, Clare felt compelled to continue the subject. If he deflected, so be it. At least she would have tried to satisfy her curiosity.

She eyed the other patrons of the tearoom. Mostly women with their friends or those they sought to impress enough to make them so, the diners enjoyed the elegant fare of scones and jams, the varieties of butter, the small sandwiches of slight greens or salmon, kippers, a little caviar for flair. Clare had eaten heartily, sampling all her favourites and enjoying every morsel. Now she eyed her plate, put down her fork, and looked at him.

He waited for her, his gray eyes sad, concerned.

"You know about our terrible discovery in the park the other night," she finally said.

He nodded.

"The police have questioned you, too, I presume."

"How are you and Mirinda faring amidst the publicity?"

"Pfff!" She had to laugh as she bent her head toward him. "You saw the polite but startled looks we received as we took our seats!"

He smiled ruefully, unable to find words.

"It is the second such mystery that has literally fallen on our doorstep."

"I know, Clare. I am so sorry to see you both in such straits."

"Luckily, we've received less attention on this one than the last. Yet, the murder is unsolved."

"Is that so?"

"Well, yes. It seems Scotland Yard doesn't consider the death of a Chinese immigrant important enough to pursue beyond the obvious."

"Oh, really? Why is that?"

"No suspects. No clues to a suspect. Whoever did this did a neat job of it." At once, she thought: *How awful to say when the way he was killed was far from neat.*

The waiter appeared and hovered over them.

John waved the man away without looking up, and blasting propriety, he took her hand into his own instead.

"What do you mean?"

"Neither the *Times* nor the other two papers revealed how he was truly killed. They simply said he was accosted and met his death swiftly from knife wounds. Well, I tell you, John, he may or may not have been accosted, but he certainly met his death rather slowly."

His face blanched. "You mean he was tortured?"

"Not exactly. At least, only mental torture while the blood pumped out of him. If his attacker assumed him dead when he left him, then he was wrong." She bristled, angry at the very idea someone could escape justice for so foul a deed. "However, I do believe the attacker assumed other things which have proven to be very correct."

"Such as?"

"He assumed the police would have little interest in a Chinese man's murder, even if it did occur in a pleasant part of Mayfair. And he was right. They don't."

"My dear, I cannot imagine a man bent on murder deliberating what the police and the Yard would do when faced with the body of a Chinese man!"

"No, perhaps not. But our murderer is very wise. Very knowledgeable. Very quick-witted."

She knew he was going to ask why so she told him.

"He killed in a manner so hideous there has to be a further explanation for it. Other than anger or fear. And if I could only discern what that reason is, I might rest more easily at night."

"My dear, why not leave that to the police?"

"Yes . . . well, I would, but they seem stymied and willing to end their investigation. After all, he seems to be no one of any import. If he were a diplomat or a businessman, they might take notice. But unlike the Japanese who send us diplomats with full portfolio and former samurai intent on imitating our business practices, the Chinese have no such men here to persuade our officials to their own importance. So, to the good men of the Yard, our murdered man must be a dockworker, a coolie."

"Let it rest, Clare. The culprit might just be another coolie, you know."

"Yes, I had thought of that. But then, what was he doing in Mayfair? Late on a Saturday evening?"

"That is a question much like a double-edged sword. In turn, what was the *dead man* doing in Mayfair on a Saturday evening?"

"Yes, well . . ." She had no answers to that, but she had speculations aplenty.

He pulled back, his eyes wide. "Oh, my dear . . . don't tell me you *know* why he was in the Close!"

"No. Only a few possibilities."

"Well," he leaned forward, "what are they?"

"Did you meet Mrs Davenport the other evening at our party?" He nodded, his eyes suddenly animated. "Yes . . . well, I thought you might have much in common."

"We do. I knew her grandfather when I was in China on General Gordon's staff during the Taiping Rebellion. Impressive fellow, old Derwenter."

"Yes, an impressed navvy who escaped ship and built an empire for himself with a network of Chinese suppliers all up and down the Chinese coast. Quite a man."

"He became head *taipan* not only because he accumulated more wealth, but also because he had more ethics." John inhaled, his eyes misting with memories. "He never ran opium, only tea and porcelains and silk. He paid his coolies well. God, how they used to swarm at the docks when he sent out runners with a call to work. *Taipan Ren Tao,* they called him. 'Great One of the People's Way.' Even the Spanish and the Portuguese *taipans* came to respect him and had to increase their wages just to keep their goods moving off the docks into the holds of their ships. The Chinese *compradores* got to like the old man, too. Their squeeze was less for him. Only for him. In the meantime, the Western customs officials developed apoplexy just thinking about the sums he rendered unto the Chinese Caesar. He never skimmed. I admired him. Greatly." He sighed and shook off nostalgia. "But tell me, what has old Derwenter's granddaughter to do with the man in the park?"

Clare sighed. "I think she knows who he is and she's not telling." She avoided the issue of Yi-an.

"Because she is partially Chinese, I am sure the police have made the same deduction. There are so few Chinese here in London, fewer than the Hindus. And peoples of like mind and culture do tend to congregate. Lee Davenport probably has staff, you know . . ."

"If that's what the Yard think, they have made a great error."

"An error? How so?"

"Yes. Because unlike many Chinese and many foreigners who take up residence in another country, Lee Davenport has no retinue with her. No Chinese staff. I know. I helped her interview and hire her current staff over the past few weeks. They are, to a man and woman, including the cook, English

116

through and through."

"Well, now . . ." He sat back and smiled. "That's most unusual. But, then, not surprising, I suppose. Lee *is* more British than Chinese."

"I know. Regardless, though, whoever came to the Close that night and met the poor soul in the park must have assumed there was another Chinese close by."

"Another Chinese who could be blamed."

"Exactly."

"Why? Why do you think that he thought there was another Chinese close by?"

"Because the way the man was killed was so—so extraordinary, I can't imagine anyone doing it without some kind of premeditation. Some unusual reason to do him in in just that way."

She suddenly caught herself and looked about her. All of these well-mannered people would scream in horror if they knew what she spoke of in their presence. Castration—at teatime—was not a usual item on their list of acceptable subjects. Nor hers, either. Clare bit her lip and looked into her lap.

"Forgive me, John. You asked me to tea and the Assyrian exhibit, and I have us discussing a most awful subject. Please, let's discuss something else."

His eyes crinkled sweetly. God, she could get to like his eyes very much.

"Shall we discuss when I shall see you again?" He gestured to the waiter to tally the bill.

"Yes, please."

"Aside from Saturday evening at Gus's dinner party? And Saturday a week, when your cousins have invited me to Julia Clively's wedding to my

117

friend the Earl of Berwick?"

She liked his perseverance, his suave demeanor. She smiled . . . or did she blush? "Yes, aside from those two events."

"Wednesday a week? For Wagner's 'Rheingold' at the Albert?"

"I see I must refresh my German."

Ten

Clare stood alone in the far alcove of the Eastern Import Company, admiring the sleek male torso before her. He was nude. Hard, black basalt. Quite athletic. Quite well en—

"My dear Lady Murdoch!"

She spun about to view the apoplectic face of the newest clerk employed in this huge shop of Eastern delights. *He* was short, thin, and—of course—dressed up to his ledgelike chin with white starch and black wool. She could not allow him to destroy, with his tendency toward Victorian prudery, her appreciation for the other man's totally satisfying figure.

"How do you do, Mr—?"

"Desmond. Mr Farnsworth Desmond," he said as he reached for the ubiquitous white sheet she had flung to the floor.

"Yes . . . well, Mr Farnsworth"—she waved an index finger at him—"do, please, leave that drapery where it is. The poor man won't die of cold, you know. And I, my dear man, won't die of shame. The torso is superb. Second century B.C., Gandhara school, I think. How do you expect to sell it if indeed you do not display it?" She walked a few paces around the pedestal and faced the front of the fluid form, which even from the back she knew represented the

119

very best of Greco-Indian sculpture. "Tell me about this piece, please."

"Oh, milady, I—I wonder if you would mind if—?" He gestured with open palms toward the front of the establishment, swallowing hard from embarrassment. "I really do not know much about anything in this room. It is for gentlemen only, surely you know, and you—"

She pressed her lips together and refrained from rolling her eyes heavenward. "Very well. Send me another clerk, if you must. I am waiting for Mr Thorne."

Desmond gulped and scurried away.

Her eyes danced with glee. He would never want to deal with her again. All the better, since she hardly ever had patience with the novice junior clerks. Clare comprehended more than they did, and she would bite her lips raw as they tried to describe artwork she knew indisputably well.

She hooked one finger in another pristine drape and let it slide to the floor.

Oh, yes. She knew so much of it so well.

Like this voluptuous Buddhist goddess Tara. Of finely crafted copper, the four-foot statue was clearly destined for a man's study or inner sanctum or, worse, some "nonexistent" back room of a men's club.

Or this Japanese woodcut print of the "Gay Quarters" of Tokyo from the Tokugawa period. She had seen not only one, but whole books of prints meant for the discerning and licentious eyes of appreciative male patrons. Of course, the works were startling in their audacity, their finite detail, but they were also some of the very best of the *ukiyo-e* style of art.

"Lady Clively-Murdoch! How lovely to see you!"

This time Clare spun about to find the man she had come to see. Tall, bald, and impeccably attired in striped charcoal-gray suiting and white linen shirt, Randolf Thorne sported a small rose boutonniere as well. A trait he had adopted after his years in Paris, where he had worked with a Dutch merchant of diamonds.

Engagingly Parisian and joyously Dutch, he clasped her hands together and kissed the fingertips. "I was delighted when the receptionist told me you were here. It has been more than a year since you have been in to see me." He stood back, folded his hands together before him, cocked his head to one side, and grinned at her. "I see you have found the most interesting of our current collection."

"Mr Thorne, I came in here to escape. You know I cannot abide the officiousness of the younger clerks. Until you have trained them, *educated* them in the works displayed, I simply cannot listen to their prattle. A few minutes ago, I was regaled with a history of how Buddhism spread from India to Japan, and the storyteller forgot to include its path through China."

He smiled, knowing she never meant any harm. "Dear lady, I should probably hire you to educate my staff. My clients would get an accurate account, I know."

She lifted her chin and grinned at him. "You would get the best bargain, too."

"I am quite sure of it. But tell me"—he came round to stand beside her as she admired a T'ang pottery figure of a man and woman in fast embrace—"how can I help you today?"

"I search for that rare item, Mr Thorne." She let her

121

eyes fall to the entwined man and woman. "The unusual, the most fitting . . . wedding gift."

He chuckled at her double entendre and her verve. "I see. Then it must be for one of your two approaching family nuptials."

"Correct."

"As you can see, I have many new items, not only in this room, milady, but also in the main showroom. As I describe the newer pieces, perhaps you can give me a few ideas as to what appeals to you—or to the brides, perhaps."

Clare harrumphed to herself as Thorne led her about. Julia, Honoria and George's daughter, was soon to marry Dominik Swinford, the Earl of Berwick, a fifty-seven-year-old man with three daughters, scads of money, and no heir. In fact, it was for the last two reasons that Julia and Dominik were to wed: she for his millions, and he for her family tradition of twins, twins, twins. At fifty-seven, he had been a widower twice before, and he had no time now for frivolities or mistakes. Meanwhile, Flo, Julia's twin sister, had given indications to Indy and Clare lately that perhaps Julia had given Dominik ample reason to believe he might find more than solace in her arms.

One thing Clare knew for certain: Julia's most treasured wedding present would be the one she would acquire because of the marriage. She wanted wealth and position. A flaming lot of both, actually. And marrying Berwick would hit the nail on the head for her. No other wedding gift would match that. So then, it really mattered not what anyone bought for Julia on this most impressive day of days; she had acquired the prize by herself. In tune with that, Clare had already sent along a silver tea service dating from Queen Anne's time.

Whereas, to acquire an appropriate present for the second Clively marriage of the summer season, Clare had to do more searching. Robin and Sarah not only made an interesting pair, but they created a superb challenge. Robin, at sixty-two, the only son of a second son, required little more in life than what he had recently attained: exoneration from a charge of murder and release from decades of dejection at a woman's rejection of his suit. The jewel in the crown of it all was his freedom now to marry the finest love of his life, Sarah Mattingly, who in return asked for nothing more than Robin himself.

So what appealed to the two brides was, by all means, irrelevant to this discussion. Randolf Thorne, standing before a carved rosewood chest "imported from Nanking, where it once belonged to a Sui emperor's concubine," did not seem to notice that Clare was not listening. He led her on to other treasures — tea sets for the ritual of the Zen ceremony, silk kimonos of gossamer weight from Kyoto, and terra-cotta figures of everyone from Confucius to nameless *literati* and the Son of Heaven's imperial entourage.

"These are quite lovely." Thorne picked up one two-inch-high figurine reverently. "Notice the translucence of the porcelain. This is the emperor's concubine and, escorting her on her palanquin, her eunuchs. Beside him are his bannermen, his personal guards. This assembly is a rare treasure, I can tell you, milady. Mr Sampson, the senior partner of Eastern Import Company, gained these on his last trip to Peking in the spring. He bought them from the Dowager Empress's personal household supplier. Of course, this figurine has to be a representation of the last emperor, not the new one. It will be quite some years before any china works can cast another entourage like this, don't you think?"

She frowned. "What do you mean?"

"I thought you would know; you seem to keep current with such news. Well, let me tell you, then. The new emperor will not have a wife or concubines to model for such an assembly as this for many years. This is, of course, if the Dragon Lady allows the little boy to live that long."

Tzu Hsi was a dragon, aptly characterized. She had been a second wife, therefore technically a concubine, chosen years ago by her husband for her beauty. Combining that with her intelligence, she had controlled her husband, both in bed and out. Producing one treasured son, when the first wife produced none, Tzu Hsi had risen from "The Yi Concubine" to greater influence.

Indeed, some said, *she* was the one who had whispered in her husband's ear from behind the bamboo screen whenever officials came to perform the kowtow of three kneelings and nine prostrations. *She* who penned imperial edicts. *She* who decided the fate of the Taiping rebels. *She* who suggested the commander of the Chinese ragtag imperial army become the hated foreigner, that white devil, the British general Charles George Gordon. *She* who approved Gordon's actions of suppressing mutinies among his Han Chinese army by personally dragging them by their pigtails before their peers and ordering them immediately shot. *She* who valued this young Western commander so that she would award him the highest honours in China, decorating him with the Yellow Riding Jacket and the

Ruby Button of the First Rank for his Confucian hat.

Thereafter, Gordon bore the dubious honour of "Chinese" Gordon, though today he was acclaimed Governor of Equitoria, with domain over the upper Nile, the Sudan, and all its khedives. He even sought to suppress the slave trade in the interior of Africa, a malicious endeavor where one African profited from another's subjugation.

Subjugation. Exactly what the Dragon Lady did best.

"May I see the emperor?" Clare held out her hand.

Thorne deposited it in her palm with great care.

The emperor, dressed in the imperial yellow that was his supreme right to wear from head to foot, was a handsome young man. Although he had succeeded to the Dragon Throne on the death of his father, Emperor Hsien Feng, in 1861, the Tung-chih emperor had never wielded power without the approval of his mother, Tzu Hsi.

"When did he die?" Clare asked, her mind racing, trying to remember newspaper accounts and hating herself for not knowing.

"The first of the year, I believe."

So that was it! She had been ill. Confined to her bed. Uncaring of news or food or anything important!

"And the new emperor is a boy, eh?"

"A *small* boy. Only three years old, they say. The son of her husband's brother. The Dragon Empress chose the child because he is the cousin of her son, the dead Tung-chih."

"But that's against Confucian principle!"

Her vehemence took Thorne aback. "It is?"

"Of course. No person of the same generation may

125

succeed an emperor because he cannot give the dead man his just honours as his revered ancestor. It is, quite simply, the worst outrage a Confucian can visit upon another."

Thorne shrugged. "Tzu Hsi has done it, custom or not."

Clare stared at the array of eunuchs and bannermen before her on the table. "How could she get them all to comply?" she asked herself.

Thorne shook his head. "She has held power for so long, many would be frightened to oppose her. Do not some still say she poisoned her husband to take back an old lover as well as put her own son on the throne?"

"Yes. Gossip in China runs rampant. Even the newspapers inside the Settlements could not report a confirmed story of the doings in the Imperial City. Tzu Hsi and her son, the Tung-chih emperor, had so bound up the City in regulations, few dared to request an audience with them except for the most important issues."

"It is a pity. A great empire ruined."

He paused.

She pondered the entourage.

"Shall I leave you to consider them, milady?"

She blinked up at him. He meant, did she wish to purchase them.

"I am considering it, Mr Thorne. Considering it . . . . Really, when I came in, I had in mind an ivory chess set or a pair of fu dogs, perhaps."

"Two wise choices as wedding presents, but I regret to say I have neither. Mr Sampson is returning to Foochow and Tientsin this September, however. If you still wish such items, I will be happy to add them to his list."

"Thank you, Mr Thorne, but as you might well understand, I need these items before then."

"Very well, milady."

In those few words and from his eyes, she knew he understood her fascination with the tiny figurines was separate from her need for appropriate wedding gifts.

"I wish I might have been able to help you."

Clare smiled pleasantly and made her way out of the shop. The day was bright, warm as June days promised. But she felt no brightness or warmth, because she had learned nothing of any use.

She turned south for the Ballantine Emporium. Certainly, there she would have more luck with fu dogs, if not information.

"Fu dogs," Henry Ballantine ruminated, one forefinger on his white goatee. "I am most sure I *do* have a pair of fu dogs . . . Yes, yes, most sure." He drifted backward into his alcove office. "Wait, wait. Right there, milady. I—" he waved a hand in excitement, "I must check my records."

From her position before the shop's inner door, Clare could see him march to his massive desk, battered as if it had been at sea with Nelson, for God's sake. He leaned over, his voluminous middle sagging toward his overladen desktop, the necessity of turning the pages of the ledger requiring him to button his coat and constrict his stomach muscles.

He licked his forefinger and thumb to turn a page. "I knew it! Of course, I have one . . . two . . . three pair." He smacked his lips and looked at her over his rimless eyeglasses. "Just brought them in on our latest shipment." He squinted and let his lips mutely deliver a soliloquy. "Yes, yes."

He walked out, beaming, and faced her. "I have three pair. All at my factory on the docks. My assistants are unloading the latest cargo today and tomorrow. I would say it would take me . . . oh, perhaps two or three days to uncrate them and find this particular portion of the shipment. As usual, the shop is closed Monday. Might you be able to wait until, say, Tuesday, Lady Murdoch?"

"Tuesday . . ." She feigned displeasure, stalling for time and information. The fact was she had not planned on receiving such prompt service here. She had expected that the usually unavailable Mr Ballantine would perform his normal function of preoccupied or absentee proprietor of his Ballantine Emporium. She had very rarely received his personal attention and ordinarily counted on the reliable assistance of his knowledgeable underling, who today was ill.

She looked displeased. "I really do wish to make a selection soon. Because of my illness this past winter, I am very late in selecting such gifts. You can understand my need to find the very best."

"Oh, yes, indeed, I do. Why not have a chair and rest while I describe the pairs for you?"

"Oh, can you?"

She took the chair, an overstuffed affair with weak innards and old, sharp wire springs that made her twitch. Between her and Mr Ballantine stood a glass-topped display table, inside of which small, priceless items sat encased in crimson velvet.

She plopped her silver chatelaine on her lap, pulled off her gloves, and smiled at him. "Please do tell me what they look like."

He pulled up a chair opposite her at the table, crossed one leg over the other, and combed his goatee—which didn't need it—with his four fingers.

"The first two are Ming, five or six inches tall. Blue and white. Delicate carving despite the bold colours."

"Precisely. Celadon is a much finer Ming product."

"Agreed." His dark brown eyes wrinkled in a small smile. "Many of my customers have not such an intricate knowledge of the Orient, milady. But I have something for everyone. The other two pair should interest you more."

He shifted, crossing the other leg now. "The second pair are from Loyang. Very large and heavy. Two feet tall and perhaps two stone. Black and white with gargoyle expressions. Very lionlike, but fierce. Imitative of the eighth-century period."

"They sound impressive, Mr Ballantine, but I don't want to frighten the bride and groom, just wish them long life and happiness."

He grinned. "I do understand. The third set is contemporary Ch'ing. Fifteen inches tall. Vermilion with a bit of yellow and green on kaolin china clay, with a *flambé* glaze and inset obsidian stone eyes. Very nice for a drawing room piece. Very unique. In fact, they come from the same pottery factory in Peking which the Dowager Empress uses to supply her personal household."

"Is that so?" Clare felt her heart give a leap. Here was her opening to gain gossip, even if more political news was not quite what she sought. "I understand she has many troubles these days."

He snorted. "Trouble seems to follow the woman."

"Yes, I know. I lived in Hong Kong and Shanghai when her husband, the old Hsien Feng emperor, was alive. My husband and I even lived through the Taiping assault on Shanghai in '53 and '54. Do you know there is an old saying among the Chinese that the empire will fall when a concubine controls the throne?"

"Is that so?" He chuckled. "I do believe it, I do. She has surely taken matters into her own hands since her son died in January. Now she has a little boy, her nephew, on the throne again, and once more, she will not need to share the power with any other woman."

"Oh, you mean her sister-in-law, the First Empress, is dead?"

"No, no. The First Empress still lives, but then, she was never a challenge to Tzu Hsi. I mean that the Tung-chih emperor's young wife died, three months after him." Ballantine examined his nails. "Some say the young woman committed suicide. I would say they'd be right about that. I would rather die than face the wrath of old Tzu Hsi.

"It is said old Tzu Hsi was so jealous of her son's attentions going to his wives that she often invented misdemeanors just to have the eunuchs hold them down and beat them with a bamboo rod! If she did that to the emperor's wife, no wonder the woman committed suicide. Of course, some others say worse and claim Tzu Hsi poisoned the woman. I tell you, Lady Murdoch, that country deserves to fall. The woman is a witch."

"She does not seem to realize the world is changing."

"I should say! She causes real problems for us all by her infernal—excuse me, milady—her terrible dedication to the past. Silk costs rise. Porcelain's not so bad. Lacquerware . . . well, sometimes, it is better for me to buy from other merchants in Malay or Calcutta than it is for me to make my journey to China and expect to get good prices."

Clare glanced about appreciatively. His walls were full of *shojis,* scrolls, fans, and mirrors with gilt edges. His shelves were full of Japanese *haniwa,* samurai swords, Burmese ivory pagodas, Bombay brass candelabra, and Liu-Ch'ou lacquerware. His case, here before her, sported gold necklaces with pearls and rubies, an emerald-studded dagger, and two four-inch-long nail covers. The type Chinese *literati* wore—and with which they never parted.

She smiled. "Mr Ballantine, I think that as always you have amassed a wonderful collection of Oriental goods. Rare and quite amazing. Why, if I were a collector, I would certainly acquire these nail covers. Where did you find them?"

"Do you like those?"

Yes, indeed she did. They sparked memories of one set of hands, once pampered and manicured, later unmoving among the impatiens in Clively park.

"I have never seen any quite like them."

"I hadn't, either. That's why I bought them."

"A Confucian *literati* sold them to you?"

"Oh, no. A Chinese man, though, to be sure."

Clare sat forward. "Did you buy them here in London?"

He frowned at her, looking her over for a long time before he spoke. "Yes, I did. Why?"

"Oh," she shrugged, trying to appear nonchalant, "I simply wondered how one might acquire such wonderful artifacts."

She knew it best if she prepared to go, creating a diversion for her real interest. She smoothed her pink silk walking skirt and pulled on her gray lace gloves.

Composing her features, Clare smiled pleasantly at him. "He spoke English, I assume."

Ballantine, who had busied himself with unbuttoning his snug suitcoat, glanced at her. "Who?"

"The Chinese man who sold you those."

"Oh, yes. English. To be sure."

Odd. "Pidgin English?"

He smirked. "What else do they speak?"

"Yes, quite. Did he seem quite young?"

Clearly, Ballantine found this conversation not only boring but the epitome of coddling a female customer. He stretched his mouth in a smoldering smile. "Young, yes. Poor. And in need of money. Quickly. But the quality was indisputably superb. I could not refuse."

"Yes, I would not, either."

"Would you like to see them more closely?" he asked, thinking now she might truly want to purchase them.

"Yes," she lied, "I would."

He reached inside his vest pocket to extract a tiny key and unlock the glass top.

Made of intricately carved ivory, the two spanned the diagonal of her palm. "They are simply breathtaking."

"I thought so, too."

"He must have been in severe need to part with them," she murmured.

"Ah, yes."

She fingered the ivory, rolling them one way and then another to view the delicately carved phoenix and bamboo grove the covers depicted.

"Did he appear to be in good health when you saw him?"

132

That question struck Ballantine as very odd. He blinked a moment or two before he said, "Yes."

"Would you know him if you saw him again, Mr Ballantine?"

"No, milady. I am sorry to say I would not. I knew the product. I knew he wanted to sell. Those are the only criteria I needed to know."

"Yes, well," she sighed and smiled, returning the two ivories to his palms. "Thank you, Mr Ballantine. You have been more help than you know. I shall return Tuesday for my fu dogs, sir."

Eleven

"My God, Clare! What are you doing?" Mirinda stepped gingerly around the mounds of crushed and crumpled papers here, there, and everywhere in Clare's parlour.

"Drawing," Clare muttered, munching on another scone from the tray Hopkins had left atop her japanned end table.

"And nothing pleases your particular eye, I see."

Clare caught her twin's look of tolerance and sighed. "I do try to punctuate it with a little music." She motioned to the open piano, where score sheets of her own compositions were spread all over, falling onto the cartouche carpet. "But not much is working. I must resurrect something from my brain and discover what bothers me."

"Well," said Indy with a flourishing sink into the settee's cushions, "mustn't we all!" She reached across to take a scone, examining it, nibbling a corner away, then tucking it in a napkin, away from temptation. "What especially bothers you, my dear?"

"Lee Davenport did not come to tea today."

Mirinda's brows shot to her hairline. "And?"

Clare reached for another scone, waving it in the air, her mind back to the sketch pad before her. "Nothing."

At that moment, Clare's parlour door opened with a squeak of its old hinges and Ian walked through.

"Hello, Mother. Aunt." He kissed them each on the cheek and took one of Clare's scones. "No supper yet. Do you mind?"

No one answered him. No one had minded for years and years that he ate them out of pantry and larder and never lost his slim, athletic form.

Mirinda eyed him. "If I didn't know better, I would say that you and your mother must be related. The two of you eat as if tomorrow will never come and never gain an ounce. Whereas I—"

"Look divine, Aunt." Ian winked at her as he sank down beside her, then passed Clare's tray of scones. "Have you had supper, Mother? If so, I can have Drummond ring belowstairs for the remains. Otherwise, I guess I—"

"Yes, I ate. There is a bit of lamb and roast potatoes." She winced, her mind back on her drawings.

Mirinda gave Ian a wide-eyed look of resignation and muttered, "I think we must not worry over your mother. She is mired deep in the musings of her brain. Seeing clearly," she chuckled, "requires thinking clearly, hmmm? But do tell me, Ian, how comes the investigation of the murdered man in the park? Any suspects?"

"Not a thing. No suspects. No murder weapon. Least of all, no motive. Confounded terrible, I tell you. One thing we might take a bit of pride and comfort in is that Bloom says the Dawes brothers did a perfectly wonderful job of questioning the Close tenants and our guests."

"Hmm," Mirinda crossed her arms and grimaced. "And I do hope they won't do it again. What about

Fleming, their superior? What does his report say? Have you seen it, or does Bloom keep it for his eyes only?"

"Really, Indy!" Clare had evidently surfaced from her introspection to listen to her stepson's recitation. "You know Ian shouldn't be talking about such things."

Indy mashed her mouth together. "Sorry. I am very wrought up over this. Income, you know. The bankers. Don't mind me, my boy." She patted Ian's knee and began to rise.

"Gad! Indy, please sit down. I did not mean to insult you and send you away!" Clare dropped her pencil and paper to her lap. "Ian, is there *anything* you can tell us with impunity?"

He shook his head. "I am afraid to say you know it all. Bloom says we are at a complete stop. *Fini. Punkt.*"

Mirinda grinned. "I bet the redoubtable Bloom does not say *Punkt!*"

Ian chuckled and reached for another scone. "You're right, Aunt. He knows only Russian. *Punkt* is not his ken."

"Punkt! Punkt!"

The three of them looked from one to the other.

Only Clare glanced away to the parrot in the tall oval cage in the far corner by the piano, craning her neck around the potted palm to peer at him.

For the first time since he had come through the door four days ago, she examined him minutely. And he—if indeed, he was a *he*—did the same to her.

"Punkt?" she asked of him.

"Punkt!" he replied.

"He speaks German?" asked Ian of Mirinda, who shrugged.

"He speaks!" wondered Clare.

"But *where*," asked Mirinda, "did he learn German?"

Clare rose and moved closer, squinting at the red and green feathers, the yellow head. The black eyes. Which were now on her. "Where did you learn *punkt?*"

"*Punkt! Punkt!*"

"Pfff!"

"Pfff!"

Mirinda gaped, then collapsed on the settee, holding her sides with laughter.

Ian had to inspect, of course.

"I don't think this is funny," said Clare at her grinning son.

"Mother, really." He handed the bird a scone through the wires. "He is quite talented."

"What else can he say? God knows where the bird has been. Or with whom."

"Oh, well, you can't expect that Paul asked for the bird's itinerary before he bought him."

"Bought him?!" Clare pulled her chin into her neck and glared at her stepson. "Paul told me he got him in Peru. He told *you* he bought him?"

"No, not precisely. Still, there's no telling where the animal has been or with whom."

"Exactly my thought," Clare mourned. "What a mess. Gad."

"Gad! Gad! *Punkt! Punkt!* Awk! Awk! Gad! Pfff!"

"Oh, for heaven's sake!" Clare stomped to the bell-pull by the piano and rang furiously for help.

When Hopkins rushed in, maroon as unpeeled beets, he found two very amused people and one angry one.

"Mum, what is it? Are you ill?"

Clare extended a long arm and an accusatory finger at the offending bird. "Take that creature away! Now, Hopkins! He is quite unnerving."

"He is, mum?" Hopkins saw only a sedate bird. But knowing an order was an order, he reached for the hook at the top of the wire cage.

"Yes, he is."

"But, mum, what *has* he done?"

"Talk," said Mirinda.

"Squawk," said Ian.

"Rattle on and *on!*" added Clare. "Take him away."

"Awk! Talk! Squawk! Take him away!"

Hopkins practically dropped the cage as the grating contralto boomed around the room. "My word!"

"My word! My word! Gad! Pfff!"

Clare melted onto the piano stool. "Oh, *puleease,* Hopkins, take him out. He's destroyed my train of thought. I will never be able to understand now."

"Yes, mum. Of course, mum." He hoisted the cage high and made for the parlour door. "He has never talked for us downstairs. I wonder why he started now?"

Hopkins made it to the door, which he began to close, just as the multi-coloured bird began to hop around the cage and bellow, "Set the table, Patsie. Get the salt, Louise. Trim the sails, me maties. Fire in the hole. Awk! Talk! Gad. Pfff."

"Oh, my!" he exclaimed, and then the door closed on the wreckage that was a startled Hopkins.

Indy was by now doubled over in glee.

Ian sputtered, knowing full well his mother would have his gizzard for breakfast if he didn't straighten up. "It might"—he tried valiantly to have a serious face—"be something he ate."

Clare glowered at him. "Such eloquence, you will pardon the term, is hardly poor digestion, Ian. He learned all those statements somewhere."

Indy managed a breath. *"Here,"* she blurted out, "is where he learned most of them, Clare."

"The only thing I can say is it is a very good thing puppies don't tell tales," Clare told her sister.

"Isn't it?" Indy's eyes twinkled.

Gigantic yellow scarves wound round her. Her wrists were tied, her ankles wrapped. Her body held down by laughing women. Her back stung once, twice, three times, and more, from something long and fierce, with the splice of a thousand tiny knives.

She was crying. Pleading.

A banging began. Once, twice, more . . .

She cried out and sat up in the bed.

The banging continued.

What—?

She shook her head to clear it of her nightmare.

Hopkins's voice rose up through the floorboards.

Hopkins was talking to someone at the front door.

A woman.

Clare felt for her slippers at the right side of her bed and pulled on her long emerald wool dressing robe she'd come to use since last winter. Swirling her long braid of hair out of the robe's lace collar, she flung open her bedroom door and took the hall and stairs at a run.

Hopkins met her, three steps down. "My lady!"

"Yes, Hopkins." Clare tried to peer around him and down the shadowed hall to the front door, but she could not decipher who stood there.

"It's Mrs Davenport, mum. From Number 20, mum. She says she must see you. I told her you were—"

"Yes, yes, Hopkins." Clare was already tying her sash and walking around him. "I will see her."

Lee Davenport looked as though the devils of this world and the next had pursued her from her door to this one. Without shawl or cloak, black eyes ravaged, black hair wild, mauve dress wrinkled and spotted around the white apron she wore atop, she bit her dry lips. Her complexion in the low gas flame was sallow, her eyes hollow, haunted.

"Lee," Clare beckoned to her with open arms, and the young woman rushed into them, trembling with burgeoning tears. "Come into the parlour, Lee. Hopkins, get me some tea. Bracing, please."

"No," Lee muttered, shaking her head violently.

"Yes." Clare sent her man off with a lift of her jaw, then steered Lee into the parlour and shut the door.

Both hands on the knob, she faced her visitor. The Minton mantel clock was about to strike three.

"What do you need, Lee?"

"Help. Help. You must help me. Yi-an, my cousin, began her lying-in this morning. She is in terrible pain. She faints occasionally and bleeds heavily now. At times, she cannot breathe correctly. I fear for the baby and her, too. Please, Clare. I have come for the female doctor you told me you know."

"I will send my man. Mind you, it will take him some time at this hour of the morning. If the doctor is

140

not readily available, you and I will have to continue to help your cousin as best we can. But frankly, you look as though you cannot help a soul, my dear."

She walked over to Lee and ran a hand through the silk tendrils of her unruly ebony hair. The woman pressed her face into Clare's side and gave way to sobs.

"There, there, you must be strong. Is this why you did not come to tea today?"

Lee nodded and swallowed hard on sniffles. Her tear-streaked face rose to Clare's. "Forgive me, Clare. I could not leave her. She knows no one here in London and she is so afraid. I cannot let her die, Clare. She is too important to me and so many others. My Chinese ancestors will forsake me if I let her die. She is *my* responsibility."

"Yes, my dear. I see that. From the start, I did see that." Clare smoothed Lee's hair back and cradled her close. "Tell me about the labour. When did it start and how?"

"This morning about ten o'clock. At first the pains were light, but I insisted she go to bed."

"Did she?"

"Yes. She is very frail. Fragile. Pampered and un-used to pain in any form."

Hmm. Yes, Clare saw that.

"This is her first child, I assume?"

Lee closed her eyes and nodded. "She lost one to a miscarriage, so she has all the more reason to be frightened."

"Especially if her husband is dead. She knows the temerity of life, two-fold."

Hopkins knocked once, and at Clare's beckoning, he pushed open the parlour door. His hands held a small tea tray.

"I brought a draught of brandy, mum. Hope you don't mind, but I thought Mrs Davenport might be in need of it."

"Thank you, Hopkins. Not a bad idea. Set it there on the tea table, if you please. Now, please get me some writing paper and a pen, Hopkins. I shall have to ask you to go out into the night to bring us back Dr Blackwell from her surgery or her home above it. Take a hansom, if you can hail one at this hour of the night. I shall be at Mrs Davenport's. Do not wake my sister, but inform her at breakfast where I am and what has transpired."

Hopkins inclined his head in agreement and disappeared.

Meanwhile, Clare was pouring tea into a Spode cup and handing it to her visitor. "Would you like the brandy, my dear?"

"No. I want to be at full faculty when Yi-an needs me. I am the only one who speaks Mandarin, you see."

Clare smiled woodenly and bade her visitor drink her tea, while she donned a serviceable dress and cloak.

Clare closed her parlour doors on the terrified Lee, fortifying herself to justify her coming deception. After all, if she were to gain any clue that might clarify her suspicions, she knew it best to say nothing of her own rudimentary and neglected, but serviceable knowledge of Mandarin.

The sight that met Clare's eyes made them water with grief for the young woman before her. And with grief for memories of herself in a similar state.

In a large four-postered Chinese teak carved bed on the third floor of Lee Davenport's house lay a pain-wracked young woman. Surrounded by three upstairs maids who seemed paralyzed with fear, Yi-an strained every muscle in her tiny body with her exertions.

From the looks of the room, those exertions had been many and futile. Basins of water awaited transport belowstairs. Melting ice swam in a smaller basin. Crumpled, blood-stained linens were piled in a heap on the floor by the door.

Meanwhile, the young woman lay, knees up beneath far too many blankets, propped against innumerable pillows, a twisted yellow cord between her teeth, stretched taut by her own hands. She bit the cord with bared white teeth, her face a mask of agony. Then, smoothly, as if letting water leave the skin, she let the cord drop, her teeth open, her face relax, her body go limp.

Clare felt a gasp rise in her throat, and she held back the terror she might have conveyed. *Of course, Clare. What could you expect? That this Chinese woman would abandon her own practices as she crossed from her country, her culture, to another?*

Lee, who in the bright gaslight of the bedroom seemed more coherent than in Clare's parlour, gathered up her soiled skirts, rushed to Yi-an's side, and took one of her hands to stroke it. In Mandarin, she asked, *"How are you? Do the pains come any faster?"*

"As strong, Honoured Friend," the woman replied in a mellow voice, thin as a violin string.

"You must not worry any longer, Honourable Yi. As I promised, I have brought my friend. She may be a white barbarian, but she knows of us, of the Great

143

Middle Kingdom, and she has great veneration for our ancestors and for yours, especially. She has called for the woman healer, her friend. Barbarian physicians can cure, Honourable One. I have been cured by them myself from time to time. Your pain is about to end."

But at this, the woman burst into tears, shouting *"No, no! Never to end! Pain is my fate, Noble Li."*

Lee had all she could do to gather the young woman into her embrace, smooth her hair from her face, and croon words to her that came so fast Clare could not translate verbatim, but which her heart fully understood.

Of course, through the next three hours of pain and tears — and finally joy — Clare came to completely understand that whatever else Yi-an was, she was no cousin to Lee Davenport.

Twelve

"She is sleeping peacefully. So is the baby," announced Dr Elizabeth Blackwell as she rolled down her sleeves, buttoned the cuffs on her shirtwaist, and allowed Lee Davenport's footman to assist her with her dining chair.

Clare smiled at the addition of this third person to their twosome. Lee Davenport and Clare had spent the wee hours of the morning with the handsome, hale and hearty doctor. Like herself and Lee, the lady who had delivered Yi-an of her baby looked exhausted. Yet, she had remained behind while the other two descended and finished directing the upstairs maids how to tend to the new mother. Still, the way the doctor surveyed the courses on the sideboard told Clare the good woman was starving.

Lee eyed her guest from her position opposite at the head of the dining room table. "You are quite sure she is in no danger?"

"Quite." The doctor let her kind but weary eyes tell the tale. "Thank you," she murmured to the footman as he finished pouring her tea and she took up the brew for a long, hearty drink.

"It has been a long night, Dr Blackwell." Lee motioned to the same footman to serve her guest from the sideboard, instead of the lady rising to do so herself. "I cannot tell you how much I appreciate your services."

"You are quite welcome, Mrs Davenport. The young woman did need the attention of a physician. It is true that if you had not summoned me or another doctor, she would have died. Perhaps the child, too. Thank you," she again said to the footman, who laid a heaping plate of bacon, eggs, and creamed baby potatoes before her. As she took up her fork, she glanced at Clare. "You knew she was in dire difficulty, did you, Clare?"

"The bleeding was excessive. Even before I saw the discarded linens in the birthing room, I knew from Lee that the mother fainted and had trouble breathing. That is not normal. I know because I lost two children myself in much the same manner. One was breech. The other presented oddly, too." The placenta had been delivered first and her second child, this one a girl, had been stillborn. "I am so glad you were able to deliver Yi-an of her son."

Doctor Blackwell attacked her breakfast with gusto, swallowed some, and smiled wanly. "He is a beautiful boy. Perfect in every way. Strong heart. Good reflexes. Yi-an must be a very healthy woman to have survived a sea voyage from China to England in the last trimester of her pregnancy and not have suffered from malnutrition or seasickness."

Clare continued with her food, eyes on the linen tablecloth. Here was the crux of her own suspicions.

"Yes, she is," said Lee Davenport, reaching for the marmalade jar and offering some to Clare, who declined but passed it on.

Dr Blackwell continued her own train of thought. "Yi-an is a very intriguing woman, Mrs Davenport."

"Yes," Lee said, evading the issue with a broad smile and offering her guests a plate of toast, "isn't she?"

Clare took two slices and passed it on.

The doctor accepted one piece. "What I would like to know, please, is how she came here?"

"By ship. With a friend." Lee looked at no one, staring at the opposite wall. "They came by Japanese freighter."

"Japanese . . . interesting. Well, I suppose that is normal, because the Chinese have no merchant marine, do they? But the Japanese carefully control theirs, don't they? I say in the bargain, they must serve good food on board." Dr Blackwell chuckled and munched on a corner of her toast. "Yi-an rested most of the journey, I would say. Otherwise, my dear Mrs Davenport, your cousin would have delivered this baby much sooner, with much more disastrous results. And God knows, out to sea with Japanese seamen, how much she would have suffered had she not been shepherded appropriately. She is fortunate. Does she speak Japanese?"

"No, no," Lee shook her head, frantically swallowing.

"How, then, did she communicate with the seamen? Did her friend speak Japanese?"

"No. He spoke only Mandarin."

He spoke only Mandarin. He.

Clare shifted in her chair, watching, waiting . . .

Lee recovered herself. "The Japanese sailors speak Mandarin. They have known our language for many centuries, you see."

"Interesting." Blackwell took another sip of tea, her square jaw flexing. "Well, whoever spoke what language, Yi-an has survived this travail because of her friend and your efforts. Never doubt it. You should be pleased with yourself, Mrs Davenport."

Lee glared at the doctor and visibly relaxed at the polite innocence she saw on the physician's face. "Thank you."

Clare could almost feel Lee's relief sweep around the room like a summer breeze.

Dr Blackwell ate in silence for a few moments and then lifted her eyes to Lee. "But one thing still bothers me about your cousin, Mrs Davenport. Do you have any idea why she would appear overjoyed at her baby's first cries, only to take him into her arms, unwrap him from his blankets, stare at his body — particularly that part of him which declares he is male — and weep?"

Lee shuddered as if the summer breeze had suddenly turned into a winter gale. The chill froze her features. "Male children are prized in China, doctor."

"That I know."

"Girl children, born to families which already have one and are poor, are considered burdens. Many are often left outside to die of exposure. Yi-an weeps tears of joy that her baby is a boy."

"That, alone as she is, she does not have to kill her baby girl? Is that it, Mrs Davenport?"

Forthright as Lee was, this was much too indelicate for her. She blanched. "I do not know what you mean, Doctor."

"Whatever the differences in our cultures, Yi-an does not appear to be a woman thrilled at the birth of this boy. No, I would say she would have been more pleased if he were a girl. Or is her misery based on the fact that her husband is dead and her male friend is no longer here to assist her? He isn't, I assume. Is he? I mean, I have not seen him."

"You are correct. He is not here. She is alone. She has only me. Only me to help her now. And in China," Lee seemed to rally, "one woman relying on another is not as secure a relationship as a woman relying on a man."

Clare's and Elizabeth's gazes met and held. Yet, it was the doctor who said, "A woman without a man, even in England or the United States, must traverse rough waters, Mrs Davenport."

Lee nodded. "Naturally then, you can understand Yi-an's distress. She is in a foreign land alone, except for the help of another woman. Not a good position for a young Chinese widow with one small baby."

"Yes, yes, Mrs Davenport. That makes perfect sense. In the meantime, she has a long convalescence in store. She lost much blood and is very weak. I would hope she would be able to nurse her baby, but unless she receives constant care, the hemorrhaging may start again. I would like to post a nurse to her care, if you don't mind, Mrs Davenport."

"Of course."

"It may be costly," added Blackwell. "I wouldn't think a woman alone has such means to—"

"She has little means, you are right. But anything she needs, doctor, I will provide her."

She is my responsibility, Clare remembered Lee agonizing in the dark despair of last night.

Dr Blackwell turned to Clare. "I was thinking that your cousin, Florence Clively, might be the perfect person for this position, Clare."

"I know she would be delighted," said Clare, wondering if Flo had finished her private duty for an ailing young countess. Even if she hadn't, Clare would do her utmost to persuade her to take this on. This was too vital. Or, to be precise, too deadly. "I can send my man round to her current position after I return home, and we shall know by noon, certainly, if she is available."

"Splendid. Well then, Mrs Davenport, with Miss Florence Clively in attendance, your cousin should recover her full strength very soon. And, whatever else may befall her, Yi-an should be proud of her own stoic performance through this ordeal and proud of her healthy son. He is a beautiful boy and will live a long, happy life."

Lee tried but could not hide the tears in her eyes as she said, "May your words be fulfilled, Dr Blackwell."

Flo stuck her nose out the servants' entrance and sniffed the morning air. Damp, as one could expect at four in the morning, but warm and promising to become warmer. Still, she wrapped her sturdy wool cloak over her crisp white uniform and ever so quietly stepped out onto Mrs Davenport's back lawn.

It was so early, so very quiet, with not even the birds singing yet. She grinned to herself, edging the hood higher over her face, and picked her way gingerly across the dewy grass toward Scarborough House. She'd crept from her bed in Lee Davenport's house, washed and dressed rapidly, checked to see her charge was sleeping soundly, and fled down the back stairs. All in an effort to sneak out before Mrs Davenport or her staff suspected she'd gone missing. After all, this was the best — and the only — time to deliver her "news."

"A bloody fugitive!" she muttered to herself as she hoisted her skirt, avoiding her second herb garden, one forgotten trowel, and a dustbin.

"Why I do this," she tut-tutted to herself and grinned, "I know full well!"

Keeping to the walls of toolsheds or dustbins, she darted from Mrs Davenport's Number 20 to the as yet unoccupied house next door. Still, she twisted her ankle on a poorly turned edge of Number 18's garden walk and cursed.

"Not ladylike to curse," she reprimanded herself, sinking back against a woodshed when one hand shot out and seized her round the waist.

The air woofed from her chest as she registered one hard, powerful body dragging her flush against his own. She used the only weapons she had—elbows and shoes.

"Ooof! Owww!" The hard body moaned and clamped her closer. "If that's the way you're going to be! . . ." He grabbed her again and came up with one sweet breast filling his huge hand.

She stomped on his foot. Serviceable lace-up shoes did a mighty job on toes.

"Ughh!" he groaned, twirling her in his embrace, bringing her breast to belly to thigh against him. "We'll see about prowlers . . ."

"It's you!"

"My Grandmother's nightshirt! It's you!" His incredulous eyes pored over her softly rounded square face and fully rounded bosom. God, she was plush. She felt even more so. He set her away at arm's length.

"Florence, for pity's sake, *why* are you roaming around the Close's back gardens, dressed like that, at this hour of the morning?"

"Ian Murdoch," she seethed, straightening her black cape and recovering her dignity, "I might ask you why you are accosting women at this hour of the morning?"

His eyes caught shadows playing across her ripe lips and her ever-so-brown, almost-black hair. She was quite simply lovely. If he hadn't acknowledged it before in daylight or gaslight, he could damn well appreciate her now in dwindling moonlight.

"Well?" she urged, feigning fury and crushing the insane urge to caress that strong, square jaw and then strangle him.

He grinned, all teeth, all flash and charm. "I was on my way home when I saw a black cat moving across the lawns. Imagine my surprise when I find the cat is"—he made a wide gesticulation with his hands and chortled—"gigantic!"

She had to grin back. But she turned on her heel and headed for the house, anyway. "I am not that big!"

No, but perhaps if you stood in my arms one more time, I might truly measure . . .

He had to run a few steps to keep up. "You didn't tell me why you are out before the morning fires are even lit."

"I have news for Clare and Mirinda."

"I know they're not awake yet. Perhaps you can share a pot of tea with me and tell me the news."

She glanced at him out of corner of her eye and allowed him to open the servants' door to the kitchen for her.

"Ah," he crooned, "Scarborough servants are up and about. Someone has already opened the door."

Flo swept past him into the kitchen, where the two scullery maids, Rose and Nancy, worked at stoking the fire in the big hearth.

Each maid dropped a curtsy and a jaw.

"Morning, Miss Clively, Mr Murdoch," they echoed, checking each other to see that they spoke together.

Ian chuckled good-naturedly and took Flo's cloak. "Don't think a thing of this, girls. Miss Clively and I met just yonder in the garden, didn't we, Florence?"

"We certainly did," Flo confirmed, and moved to the big table in the center of the room. Discarding her gloves, she glanced about. "Rose, Nancy, might I trouble you for some paper and a pen? I must leave a note for Lady Clare."

"Yes'm," Rose bobbed and hurried off, while Nancy moved to take out pots and pans for Pence to prepare the morning meal.

"Pence'll be out in a minute, miss. Want ta stay for break'ast, miss? I know you'll want some, Mr Murdoch. This mornin' Pence says we're making waffles with lots o' fresh strawberries. Ye can stay an' I'll lay a place so ye can eat 'ere if you want."

"No, Nancy. Thank you. I must get back to my charge. Oh, good, you found things, Rose. Thank you."

Flo grasped them from the young girl's hands and sat at the table to pen a letter to Clare.

"What have you discovered," Ian questioned, leaning over her shoulder, "that you had to come here this early, hmm?"

She made mischievous eyes at him and watched — both horrified and fascinated — as he froze, swallowing like a man tempted and starved.

The look left its message. He thought she was attractive. She had known it, had felt it, even the other evening at the musicale when he had fetched her champagne and dessert, regaled her with his stories of his Black Watch regiment, and generally looked like a very *un*holy angel in his sleek evening clothes.

"I don't think I should tell you," she said, and began to compose her letter in her head.

He marched around the mammoth oak table and pulled out a chair, scraping the clumsy thing across the earthen tile with a screech that made her set her teeth.

"Flo, you can tell me. I am not working on this case

153

because of my status and family ties, but I do still work for the Yard, you know."

"Yes," she muttered as she wrote a few sentences. "But you don't think your mother should be involved."

"True. This is police business and dangerous work."

"Yes." She continued to write.

"You may discover nothing."

"Yes."

"You may be wasting your time."

"Yes."

"Will you stop saying yes to me!" he thundered, slapping the thick table.

"No," she reached across the table, took his hand and passed soothing fingers over the smarting red palm. Then she looked up at him and grinned knowingly, her gently arched brows peaking over the most gorgeous set of violet-tinged blue eyes he had ever beheld.

The sight took his breath away. How could a woman look this delicious at half four in the morning? And furthermore, how could she affect one physically while speaking of spying and murder, of all bloody subjects!

He muttered vicious things under his breath.

She dropped his hand and took up her letter, folding it and tucking it into its envelope.

"What did you learn?" he asked, cradling his hand and frowning at her as she accepted a cup of tea from Nancy and drank liberally.

"Only what your mother asked me to," she said, handing her letter over to the maid to give to Clare.

"What was that?"

She cocked her head to one side and scooped up her cape, twirling it once more over her shoulders. "If I found anything strange in Lee Davenport's house."

"And you did?"

"Yes, I did."

"Flo, for God's sake, stop playing cat and mouse with me. If there is anything odd in Lee Davenport's house, I should learn of it. *I am* with the police, Flo. *You* are a nurse."

She threw him a perfunctory little smile and turned on her heel. "Yes," she said once more, enjoying the ripe irritation in his grim green eyes. She waggled her fingers at him. "Good morning, Ian."

He caught her by the arm. "Wait just a minute, Flo. You did not tell me what you discovered."

"Yes."

He rounded on her and faced her now, his broad shoulders blocking off all view of the kitchen, his virile presence obstructing flight and good judgment.

He cupped her chin and raised it so that she could not avoid the magnificent specimen of healthy man before her.

"What did you learn, Flo?"

That I should stay well away from you, old boy.

"Flo?"

She licked her lips.

"I am waiting."

"Clare wanted to know if people came and went at odd hours of the night from Lee Davenport's house."

He cocked a brow and waited for her to elaborate.

She scanned the kitchen to see if either of the scullery maids stood listening to them. Though both had gone about their business, she dropped her voice to a bare contralto.

"From what I can see, the only one who does so is the coachman, who has rather a fondness for Mr Henry's wife."

"The baker's wife?" Ian hooted. "Mr Henry in the Close shops?"

"One and the same."

"Outrageous," he mused. "I wonder what they're doing?"

Flo's delicate eyebrows shot to her forehead. "Not making bread, I'll wager."

Ian snorted. "Yes. Anything else?"

Flo flushed to the roots of her hair. "Well, I will tell you, I have no idea what else they do while they are—"

"No, no!" He chortled now, holding his breath to keep in the hilarity and not offend her further. "I mean, did you learn anything else about Mrs Davenport's house."

"Yes," she lowered her voice significantly. "Each and every housemaid under the age of good sense thinks that Burton is the most handsome man—pardon me, young man—they have ever seen. Must be that Welsh charm. In any case, they would gladly meet him anywhere, anytime, for a dalliance. And some have tried, I understand."

"My God!"

Flo nodded, once more grinning.

"What else?"

"Other things."

"Flo, I mean to have an answer. What else did you discover about the workings of Lee Davenport's house?"

"I am none too happy I did find out, I'll say. I heard Clare's reasoning and thought it thin. But I was wrong."

"Well, what is the news?"

"Lee Davenport welcomed Yi-an into her house more than a week ago. She came late on a Friday evening says the cook, who was called from her bed to prepare rice and vegetables. Mrs Davenport's personal maid tells me that she herself managed to glimpse Yi-an and her escort from the top of the stairs. The young man accompanying her was Chinese. They both were escorted into the drawing room to see Mrs Davenport."

Ian raked his hair. "My Lord. I wonder . . . And what does the butler say about them?"

"Williams has thought very little of the incident."

"But why?"

"We might conclude that Williams, the butler, would have let them into the house and that he would know what they looked like. But he doesn't. He was very ill that evening and did not answer the front door."

"Who did?"

"Mrs Davenport."

"Answered her *own* front door? Astonishing."

"Yes. Very."

"She must have known they were coming, Yi-an and this gentleman. She must have! How else would she know to wait up simply to answer her own front door?"

"Quite. Mrs Davenport emerged from her drawing room over an hour later, alone. She then told her staff Yi-an was considered an honoured guest. Evidently, Mrs Davenport thought so much of her cousin, she immediately assigned her an upstairs bedroom."

"But what happened to the gentleman?"

"Mrs Davenport told her maid he was a friend. He left, the maid says, sight unseen, before Mrs Davenport emerged from her drawing room."

"Therefore, he was not a husband or a suitor. Only a friend wishing to remain a friend."

"Why is that difficult to understand?"

"The staff cannot understand how a handsome man

and an attractive, if very pregnant woman can travel halfway around the world, depending on each other as they must have, and yet maintain a distance that makes it possible for them to take leave of each other within hours of their arrival."

"Do they not think a man may honour a woman as a friend?"

"No." She let her eyes outline his boldly sculpted features, admiring him more than she should. "Never."

"He left then and they have not seen him since?"

"Yes."

Ian fumed. Was this errant Chinese man the same man in the park? He knew this was his stepmother's conjecture.

Ian's mind raced with the possibilities. Clearly, the Dawes brothers had not questioned Mrs Davenport closely enough to learn of this visitor from afar. If they had, they might have had the foresight to ask her maid to view the corpse and possibly identify him as this mysterious companion to Yi-an. But they hadn't.

As it was, his stepmother and his aunt and his . . . well, God's blood, what *was* Flo to him? *Precious.* That's what she was. And here she was meddling in things the Metropolitan Police and the Yard and even Bloom, damn his eyes, should have pressed for and discovered by themselves!

God, if only he could have been assigned this case. Or not be a probationer! Or a Clively . . . or close to it.

"Damn!" he muttered, grasping Flo by the wrists. "If you see anything suspicious, you come straight to me, do you hear me?"

"Yes," she promised. *How can I stay away?*

Thirteen

At Gus's description of who should go in to dinner with whom, the party of fourteen dinner guests rose as one.

"I am delighted to escort you in, Mirinda!"

Blond, dashing Charles Beaumont offered Indy his arm, and she closed her emerald and pearl fan to order her skirts about her.

She smiled, taking her mind from Gus's lavish suite of Prussian blue silk settees and milky white satin chairs. Bismarck had suffered no delays nor spared any expense for the classical lavishness of his newest emissary's abode in the Langham Hotel on Portland Place. Gus was to have everything here in London. Every amenity, every assistance, and every opportunity to lead his diplomatic cohorts brilliantly.

Charles was smiling at Mirinda, patting her hand as they walked down the gilded mirrored corridor toward the dining room. "I did not have the opportunity to speak with you for very long last week at your birthday celebration."

"There were quite a few people, weren't there?" Indy allowed her hand to loop his arm casually. With a twist of her slippered foot, she fought with her wayward, voluminous satin skirts and smiled at him as they followed Gus and Lady Amarylis Sommes into the dining room.

Amazingly, though they were fourteen for dinner, frightfully young Lady Amarylis took precedence and therefore gained the right to be escorted into dinner by their host, the Prince Hessebogen.

Charles patted Mirinda's hand. "I thought Madame LaTour gave a stunning performance."

"Did you really?" Indy eyed the way Amarylis leaned into Gus's forearm, giving him ample opportunity to gauge the firmness and weight of her ample charms. *Hmmm.*

"Did you not?" Charles's pale blue eyes flashed in sheer surprise.

"I thought her rendering lovely, but perhaps she has strained her voice recently."

The same way other women strain their bodies. The same way Amarylis strains to laugh at Gus's wit. Good God, he cannot be so funny that she needs to throw that giraffe's neck out of joint, does she? The only thing she accomplishes is to give him an unobstructed view of her pink cantilevered cleavage. Just how many pounds of whalebone does she carry in that ship of state of hers? And what can her husband think of such a flirt?

Mirinda tried to contain her agony. She knew instead of truly smiling she was gnashing her teeth and baring them at pleasant Charles Beaumont. But she could not help herself. She had shared Gus over the decades with a phantom. Never in twenty-five years had Mirinda been in his presence and not been the only woman in his view.

The double doors opened and Mirinda surveyed Gus's dining room as if it contained all the charm of Newgate Prison. The creamy expanse of Corinthian columns with gilded mirrors and bronze chandeliers met eyes blinded by the evil of jealousy. She noted the full-length table, groaning with a centerpiece of wintergarden purple orchids and white carnations and green ferns, and registered absolutely nothing but her own gaudy green hostility. She commented on the beauty of the floral bouquet which swept the length of the fourteen-person table, and wished she were home, in bed, alone. *Why had she agreed to come here?*

Amaryllis Sommes, in the latest daring design of blue hydrangea pöult-de soie silk with hummingbird feather trim at her low corsage, sank into her chair to the right of Gus and absolutely gushed with gratitude, pride of place, and familiarity.

She was young. Twenty-five, if a day. Brassy blond, and blindingly so. Buxom, feigned or real, only her personal maid would know for certain. Or hopefully, her husband might, if he would dare tell any tales such as that. Because after all, this was England, where no gentleman ever discussed his wife's bounties. Not even one such as Mr Joshua Sommes, who as an untitled man had done quite well for himself by marrying Lady Amaryllis Forrester-Leigh, only daughter to the Earl of Bently and heiress to her papa's fabulous wealth from half a dozen Indian ruby mines.

Joshua's virtues had been inherited from his father and his grandfather, both of whom had held Cabinet posts as under secretaries for the Colonies and who had held the seat consecutively for Southwick for more than forty-two years. So now, at thirty-four years of age, Joshua had great prestige. But for far longer, he had possessed something much more attractive—a bold, suave manner and a comeliness that made debutantes push themselves upon him.

Finally, one day, the debutante who pushed was the Lady Amarylis, and Joshua, mindful of the lady's multitudinous physical and financial attributes, pushed back. They were married now for more than five years, and the combination of his prestige in Parliament and her money meant they were a match for each other and anyone they chose to take on.

Evidently, tonight, Lady Amarylis was taking on Gustav von Frey.

Indy sat down with a plop and had to rise again to clear her emerald satin train from beneath her. *Confounded fashion.*

"I say, Mirinda," Gus addressed her from his position to her right at the head of the table, "have you seen the exhibition at The Henworth?"

"Henworth?" she asked vacantly, plastering a smile on her face. "No. I am afraid not, Your Highness."

He delicately narrowed his eyes at her when she used his formal title, in violation of the tone he had set during his reception of them all.

"Quite astounding," said Amarylis, allowing a footman to place her dinner napkin in her lap. "Joshua and I went last week, didn't we, my dear?"

Her husband, seated to her right, had been caught off guard reading the menu at his left. Covering, he brushed the points of his heavy black mustache while his brown eyes twinkled. "Yes, yes. Delightful, too, I say. Not since viewing the winged lion of Nineveh at the British Museum have I seen better pieces from Assyria. Scintillating. Simply scintillating."

Down the table, Clare, who had swept her magnificent aquamarine silk train to her left as she was supposed to, had seated herself prettily, leaned forward, and voiced her appreciation of the collection. "I agree the curator has done a masterful job of placing appropriate pieces together."

John Newhall, to Clare's left, glanced at his cohorts one by one and affirmed Clare's view. "I do wish we could find similar treatment for Chinese and Japanese artifacts."

"Ah, well," said the Portuguese Petro Saldahna with a flourish of hands, "you know what we face there. China is the cradle of eastern civilization, but few will recognize it because so many surmise that our own Holy Lands are the cradle of *every* civilization."

"Exactly our problem with the point we debate even now," offered Charles Beaumont. "We cannot find agreement on China policy until we educate our own governments about the cultures."

Gus nodded. "Very true."

Mirinda watched Gus catch the eye of his man, the Baron von Macht, who had supervised the entry of the dinner party to the dining room and the solicitous attention of the seven footmen. Now that every one of the seven ladies and seven gentlemen had settled themselves into their Prussian blue velvet-lined chairs, the footmen marched silently across the Sakhara carpet toward the serving room and the kitchen.

The silent, dark angel who was Baron von Macht officiated by pouring the first of the wine. After that, each gentleman would find a bottle to his right to administer to his female companion on his left. Proud of Gus, proud of his accomplishments and his finesse, Mirinda once more felt bereft that she was no permanent part of his life.

Where one moment jealousy reigned, now sorrow stepped in and sat beside her. The others' conversations echoed off the walls of the lovely white and gold room.

"What I do not understand," said Brilliantine Beaumont with a Gallic shrug, "is how you gentlemen can hope to improve conditions in China if we cannot even here in England agree?"

Her husband frowned at her across the flowers. *"Ma chère,"* he bit off the words, "I have told you we must try. Our governments depend on us."

She pouted, her full lips and lambent black eyes combining with the jet-beaded, gold brocade of her décolleté gown to give her the look of the pedigreed, pampered Parisian.

"We lived in Tientsin, you know?" Brilliantine cast her long-lashed eyes to Gus.

Her appearance was plainly inviting, and Mirinda's sorrow vanished as her teeth ground together with greater ferocity. At this rate, she would be gumming her dessert!

Brilliantine was elaborating. "Only in April we returned, yes? We lived there for seven years, Charles and I. The Chinese have no love for us French, surely you know this, Your Highness?"

"Yes. I was there myself last winter. I saw for myself that the Chinese view all Westerners with distaste. Rest assured, *Madame,* the Tientsin problems are not solely French problems, and so we shall deal with similar ones in our little group."

Clare felt Charles Beaumont stiffen.

This was a very sensitive subject between the French and the Germans. Chinese riots in the French concessions of China were particularly troublesome. Brought on by the French government's avid support of their Catholic missions, the riots began five years ago in the port city outside Peking when the sisters who ran a French orphanage had taken in sick babies. Later, many of the children died of disease. When the villagers learned of the deaths of the children, they misinterpreted the cause and accused the French nuns of buying and then killing the Chinese children. Of course, it was untrue. But what hurt the French position and prestige in China hurt them all, even the Chinese.

And Clare knew Gus felt it keenly. He raised his glass to begin the meal, and she saw him disguise his dislike of the turn of the conversation with a smile and a toast. It was in all their newspapers that ever since the Franco-Prussian War five years ago, he had fought hard to persuade Bismarck to ally himself with the French — and the English — in China.

Today, Clare knew, the Iron Man of Germany was listening. He was allowing Gus to come to London, wasn't he? Allowing him to negotiate with Saldahna and Newhall. Allowing Gus to work with the impressive Charles Beaumont, who was the best authority on China the French Third Republic possessed.

Clare watched Gus surreptitiously as he rolled the white wine around on his tongue and sought to find a topic light enough for mixed company. More than that, he needed one that was not highly secret and would set Charles Beaumont at ease in this prickly conversation his wife had initiated.

Clare smiled as Gus found one.

"Charles, have you told your wife we did reach some agreement on the precedence we would take when we next go to have an imperial audience in the Forbidden City?"

Charles's eyes flicked gratefully from Gus to Brilliantine. "Gus has soothed us all by working out a new system."

Brilliantine was not impressed. "You mean you still fight for the right to go see that barbarian ogre, Tzu Hsi?!"

Clare watched Brilliantine fall back in her chair, the look of Western superiority written on her delicate dusky features. Her profligacy with money and her petulance were the causes, said Aunt Pru, of her husband's failure to progress in rank. This new appointment to this special committee with Gus and John and Saldahna was considered Charles's last chance to improve himself. Indeed, to insure such, Aunt Pru said many saw Charles going about in London alone, as he had last Saturday at their birthday celebration.

Brilliantine continued her diatribe against the Dowager Empress with more anger. "After what she has done to her own son, I would run her through myself if I were Chinese."

Amarylis sat forward, disregarding the footman who tried to serve her her soup and almost dropped the contents in her lap when she moved. Ignoring the footman's gaffe as any proper lady should, Amarylis stared at the Frenchwoman two seats away. "What did she do to her son?"

"Killed him."

Amarylis gasped. "Oh, surely! No! Joshua, tell me this is not so."

"Well, my dear, I wish I could." His brown eyes apologized to his cohorts Gus, Charles, John, and Saldahna. "But that is the rumour." His eyes went on to Leslie Maccarran and Jocelyn Singleton and their wives at the far end of the table. Maccarran was an impressive, redheaded Scotsman who was Under Secretary for Colonial Affairs. Singleton worked in the Foreign Office on Chinese issues. What's more, they were rigid about protocol and hated loose talk about international politics. "The official report is that the Tung-chih emperor died of 'the heavenly flowers,' which translated into our terms is smallpox."

"Then, how might she have killed him?"

All the men shifted uncomfortably in their chairs. Clare, who sat quietly while her footman placed her soup before her, shivered. Something about the men's movement made her think of the reaction most males had upon first hearing how the Chinese in the park had died. She picked up her soup spoon and began to eat, but could have been sipping dishwater for all she tasted.

"Poison," murmured Joshua Sommes.

"That is only rumour," John pointed out severely.

"It certainly is," Saldahana said. "It is what Tzu Hsi did after his death which is more heinous."

Clare sat enthralled. "What did she do?"

"She murdered his wife," John told her sadly.

Charles turned to her, wine to his lips. "Some say the wife was expecting a baby."

"No!"

"Oh, yes, my dear Clare," said Gus. "I am afraid so."

"But you are certain she died?"

Gus's eyes flicked about the table. Clare knew his worries: This was not exactly polite dinner conversation and he would snatch up the subject if one person appeared offended, but to a man and a woman, no one flinched. "Yes, Clare. We are quite certain A-lu-te is dead."

"But why would Tzu Hsi kill her daughter-in-law, especially if the young empress were with child? It does not make sense."

"Tzu Hsi is a harpy," shrugged Brilliantine. "I have told Charles and John this for years. Remember, *mon ami*"—she looked at Charles and John— "after the riots in the Taku Forts in '73, how she wanted both of you to appear for the kowtow, eh?" Brilliantine leaned across the table to fix Clare with a haughty look. "She wanted them to prostrate themselves before her for some silliness. They refused to go. I said then they should not."

John gazed off in space. "A Western man had been suspected of murdering a Confucian government official, and to disguise his actions, he had stripped the man's body of everything to make it appear a robbery. The peasants, who had seen a Western man enter the official's offices, demanded the man be turned over. Riots ensued, and twenty-five Chinese were trampled in the assault on the foreign legations. Charles and I, as the Western representatives of our governments in the Forts, investigated the incident. But we never found substantive evidence and found no culprit."

Brilliantine harrumphed. "The Chinese were very mad, and even today, Tzu Hsi wants an apology and reparations. But Charles and John said no then and they say no now. That is as it should be. Tientsin was the fault of the peasants. This fuss in Taku is also. Who is to say the Western man exists and is not a figment of the Chinese imagination, yes? Whatever we do, they misinterpret."

Brilliantine's words coated the room in a red glaze of discomfiture. No one moved.

Finally, Clare saw Gus set his soup spoon aside and look up at the Baron, whose eyes flicked to his men to clear the course.

Gus was distressed with this topic; Clare could see it. More, she could feel it. When his copen blue eyes rose, they locked with hers.

"One of our tasks in this group is to return to the records of the Taku murder to see if we can discern how the incident did occur. Not only Petro Saldahna, but both Charles and John were there and knew all Frenchmen and Englishmen in Taku at the time. If we can find a thread which will lead us to a Westerner, all well and good. If not, we still face Tzu Hsi's demands and must decide as a group how to deal with them. Our collective presence in China depends upon us finding a solution to the Taku murder which 'saves face' for all of us."

But Clare cared little for the explanation of this Taku murder. Instinct returned her to the murder Tzu Hsi had supposedly committed. "And I would suspect your deliberations are also affected then by the change from one emperor to another, even if he is only three years old."

Gus smiled at Clare's acuity. "Absolutely. We

169

must tread even more carefully now that Tzu Hsi worries over her power."

"What of the new emperor's mother? Is she no threat to Tzu Hsi's role as Empress Dowager?"

Gus shook his head. "No. You see, my dear Clare, the young boy's mother is extremely sickly and cannot live out the year. She is no threat to Tzu Hsi."

"Interesting," said Clare.

"Convenient," he replied. "Tzu Hsi has learned her lesson here. She could not control A-lu-te. The young empress was intelligent and some say very much in love with her dissolute husband, the Tung-chih emperor. A-lu-te, however, came from a clan of the Mongol Banners, allies of the Manchu conquerors. But the Manchu Empress Tzu Hsi has kept her power over the years because she surrounded herself with members of her own Yehonala clan, the original family unit of the founder of the Manchu dynasty. To continue to control China, she must have thought it imperative to control the young empress of the Tung-chih emperor. And she could not. Not before the Tung-chih emperor's death and certainly not afterward. A-lu-te was not only Mongol, but if she gave birth to a son, A-lu-te would usurp Tzu Hsi's role as Empress Dowager. Therefore"—Gus spread his hands wide as the footman took away his soup service—"Tzu Hsi not only killed her daughter-in-law, she also murdered every concubine in the Forbidden City."

"Every concubine?" Clare gasped.

"Yes. One hundred and twenty-two young women died at her hands last April."

Clare could barely breathe. She felt dizzy, as yellow scarves swirled in her mind. Yellow scarves from her dreams, yellow scarves from Yi-an's labour, one yellow scarf draped over the body of a dead man in Clively park. "My heavens, Gus. Do we have proof?"

"Only the accounts of two government officials who had an audience with the Empress the day after the massacre. Tzu Hsi alluded to the deaths."

"And?"

"The officials claim the eunuchs administered the poison to the women in their evening meal. By morning, all were dead in their beds."

Charles Beaumont sat mournfully eyeing his wine glass. "The eunuchs who administered the poison were said to have the responsibility for removing the bodies from the concubines' quarters and turning them over to the Manchu Bannermen for burial."

Oh, my good God! Clare's mouth fell open. Her eyes closed. Her heart beat frantically. Her vision was too powerful to deny. Too vivid to ignore.

Yi-an's face now loomed before her. The yellow scarf tied around the young woman's throat was the yellow scarf of the dead man in their park. Yes, Clare had seen this in her dream the other evening. Now she saw it here in this *voyant*. The other evening, she had not understood what her mind intricately fathomed. But now she did. Now she most certainly did.

She opened her eyes and sat back in her chair.

Gus and Mirinda had moved into some small conversation as the rest of the soup was cleared away. Charles sat morosely drinking his wine. John had engaged Rebecca Singleton and struck up a civil chord, as did the rest of the table.

And all the while the footmen served the fish course, Clare was silently ordering, in logical terms, what she had been puzzling over for days.

She smiled, a little smirk of satisfaction. Wouldn't Indy be speechless when she heard it all?

Gad, she wanted to clap. And sing.

By the time the footmen departed and it was time to "turn the table," Clare congratulated herself on knowing the identity of Yi-an and of the man in the park. She also knew why Yi-an was in England.

Clare could even make a good go of deducing why the man in the park was dead. And why he had been killed the way he had.

Yet, the knowledge brought no comfort.

It meant that Yi-an and her baby boy were in constant danger.

And so was Lee Davenport.

Fourteen

Lee Davenport grew pale as parchment. "Who told you that?" she whispered.

"No one, my dear. I concluded it myself." After walking many a hole into her carpets all day Sunday and most of this morning as she pondered the sheer improbability of it, Clare had finally decided to don her afternoon attire and simply confront the poor young woman at the four o'clock calling hour.

But Lee was having none of it. She was angry, pulling back in her chair, far from Clare and her accusations.

"Well, Clare, you concluded incorrectly."

Clare arched a brow. "I do not think so. Come now, you can tell me. What's more, I think you should, because you know my stepson is with Scotland Yard and—"

"Oh, no!" Lee clutched her throat. "You haven't *told* anyone, have you?"

Clare reached across to take Lee's hand. "No, my dear. I have not said a word to him yet." She'd told only an incredulous Mirinda all the details late Saturday evening. "But, Lee, you must—"

Lee jumped from her chair and prowled the

room like a demented creature. "You cannot *say* anything, Clare." She raked her hair, her black eyes roaming about her drawing room like a woman in a trance. "If you speak of this, word will go out. I will have to move Yi-an. She is still weak and—"

Clare sank back in her chair. "So, it *is* true."

Lee Davenport rushed to Clare's side and knelt before her. Grabbing at Clare's hands, she searched's the woman's eyes as tears began to slip down her cheeks. "Please, Clare, do not do this."

Clare threaded her fingers through the soft tendrils of hair at Lee's cheek. "My dear girl, you cannot protect this young woman alone. You must let me help you."

"I have learned the value of secrecy, Clare."

"Have you?"

Lee nodded, her tears stopped.

Time to become brutally honest. "My dearest Lee, this is no secret any longer. Don't you see? If Yi-an's presence were a secret, her companion would not be dead. Ah, yes. Someone knows who she is. And I daresay, that is *why* her companion is dead. That is why she and her baby, even you, my dear Lee, may now be the target."

"Tzu Hsi's tentacles reach even into the British Empire," Lee mourned. "I can scarcely believe it."

"Did not the young man's death convince you of that?"

"Yes! Yes! But I thought if we ignored it, pretended we were not involved—"

"Has Yi-an ignored it?"

Lee was speechless.

Clare persisted. "Yi-an cannot ignore it, I wager. The man was her friend."

Lee's lower lip trembled. "Her second cousin."

"Her savior?"

Lee began to cry openly. "Yes, her rescuer."

"And he loved her?"

"Oh, God!" Lee lay her head in Clare's lap and sobbed. "He adored her."

Clare dug out a handkerchief from her bombazine skirt pocket and dabbed at Lee's copious tears. "There, there, my dear."

"He knew, you see . . . he knew what Tzu Hsi planned. He was one of the Imperial Guard in the Forbidden City. Inside the walls during the day for duty, he was general of his Banner. The Yellow Banner."

"The Imperial Family of Yehonala," Clare murmured.

"Yes, yes. He was a trusted adviser to Tzu Hsi. So when she planned the death of A-lu-te, he knew she would not stop there. He knew Yi-an was next."

"Because she was pregnant."

"Ah, yes."

"And because she was the first concubine of the young Tung-chih emperor."

"My God," Lee pulled away and stared at Clare. "How did you learn that?"

Clare articulated with a few movements of her delicate brows. "I know the character *yi* means 'one' or 'first,' but there is another which is given to the first concubine. It means 'virtuous.' The conclusion was obvious."

"But I told you she was my cousin."

"My dearest, I knew from the moment I looked at her she was no member of your family. No

175

woman among you still has bound feet. And Yi-an's were teetering on Manchu—not Chinese—slippers. I also heard her speak—in Mandarin, not Cantonese. Then when she did speak, it was with great authority. Great royalty, if you will. Then of course, you gave a great piece of information away when you told me no man could touch her. No man save her husband. Who in China, I asked myself, cannot be touched by any man? Only a woman of the imperial household. I knew too much of your language and your culture for you to totally deceive me."

"Even that does not tell you of Lo-wu's connection to her."

"Lo-wu was the young Bannerman's name, eh? Yes, well, I will tell you, it was he—or rather his body—which gave me the best clues to his identity. Of course, I did not fully piece it together at the time. The yellow sash tells the most important tale."

"Yes, it is his sign of rank in the Imperial Guard. Among the Manchu Banners, the Yellow Banner is the first, the most important. Lo-wu's sash was his birthright. He would never part with it."

"Yes, Lee. I should have recognized it as a sign of his office, but I had only heard of the Bannermen, never met one. No, it was something else which gave me a clue. I knew from his build he was wellborn. I thought, naturally, he was Han Chinese. But I was so wrong. The one indicator he gave of that should have struck me first. But of course, I was so intent on proving how he was Chinese and not Japanese or some other type that I ignored the obvious."

"Which was what?"

Clare smiled and smoothed Lee's hair back over her shell-like ears. "My dear, he had no queue."

Lee shrank away, horrified. "Oh, my Lord. I thought it would not be noticeable!"

"It gave away his identity—or would have—to anyone who has spent any time in China. Only true Han Chinese wear the queue, their sign of outrage at the hegemony of the hated Manchu hordes. It marked Lo-wu, my dear Lee. Made him stand out immediately to anyone who knows Chinese society. And of course, his Chinese pyjamas gave him away. Anyone could spot him easily. Anyone, as I said, who knows Chinese society. Poor Lo-wu. He evidently thought Tzu Hsi would not pursue him and Yi-an to the ends of the earth."

"You are right. He thought he had executed his plan perfectly. Smuggling her out of the Forbidden City in a donkey cart. Changing her attire and burning her court robes in Tientsin. Meeting my cousin, the *taipan* of Taku port, and hiding on his ship until they sailed into Hong Kong. Boarding a freighter out of Yokohama to sail to London. Yes, that night when he brought Yi-an here to me, Lo-wu told me his remarkable story. He thought he was safe, and Yi-an, too. It was I who persuaded him to leave Yi-an, if only for a few weeks. I knew Tzu Hsi would send out her spies. Her hirelings. I knew she would. But at times, I am not sure it could be Tzu Hsi."

"Why is that, my dear?"

"Confucianism reveres the wholeness of the body. To go to one's death dismembered is a terrible fate.

177

And then there is the other fact"—she swallowed hard—"that the punishment for seducing an imperial concubine is not emasculation but decapitation."

"My heavens . . . But to find whoever it was—Westerner or Chinese—who killed Lo-wu, if indeed, he is still here in England, we must know more about Lo-wu's actions after he left you that night."

"He went to the docks. He said he had talked to the captain of the Japanese freighter on which he and Yi-an had sailed here, and the captain promised to hire him to help unload his cargo. Lo-wu said he would work for a few weeks and return occasionally to see Yi-an."

"It is as I thought. His body had numerous bruises about the shoulders. He was carrying cargo in the East End."

"He wanted to learn more English and make his way here. He planned a quiet life for himself and Yi-an. When she was delivered of her baby, he planned to take them to some small town and live quietly, where Tzu Hsi could not find them."

"But, Lee, how did he expect to live in a small town? He had no money, did he?"

"Oh, but he did. He was a rich man in Peking, Clare. Very rich. But he was willing to give up everything he had to save Yi-an and her baby. He loved her and would do anything for her, even forsake his family, his position, his honour, and his country. He had enough money to bribe other Bannermen in Peking so that he could smuggle Yi-an through the gates. And he told me he would soon have more. You see, Clare, he had taken his own treasures with him from his estate in the Imperial City. How he smuggled them out and Yi-an, too, I shall never know. But he did. In any case, he said the sale of his artifacts would bring him a goodly sum."

Clare remembered the items she had recently seen at the Eastern Import Company and at Ballantine's. Yes, Lo-wu had been correct: There was a great market for Oriental artifacts. A burgeoning market for . . .

"What did Lo-wu have to sell?"

"I—I do not know if I remember."

Clare gripped Lee's hands fiercely. "It is very important you remember."

"Why?"

"Because . . . perhaps he tried to sell something priceless and word spread. Or the buyer became greedy and wanted more for less. It happens, you know. Now think. What did Lo-wu have with him?"

Fifteen

Fu dogs. Clare straightened the jacket of her rose linen walking suit and adjusted the cream lace cuffs at her wrists, wishing she were simply purchasing fu dogs. Then her heart wouldn't be racing and her head pounding.

She stuck her parasol into the sidewalk and caught a glimpse of herself in the green-trimmed, small-paned windows of Fortnum & Mason, grocers to the Royal Family. She considered their unparalleled tea display while she considered the cut of her figure.

Not good. Not bad. She still had some eating to do to fill out her proportions once again.

"Later," she promised herself as she spun away from the windows and noticed a distinguished-looking gentleman admiring her from the corner of Piccadilly.

One does approach complete daffiness, Clare dear, when one speaks to one's self on street corners.

But for now, there was nothing for it but to square her chin and get on with the distasteful aspect of ferreting out information from Mr Ballantine. She had walked here from home, to get her blood surging and to focus her mind fully on the hideous task before her. With her hopes set firmly on resolving as much as possible of the mystery of who killed Lo-wu, she would see this through to the end before she had to tell everything she knew to Ian.

Clare turned toward Jermyn Street. She would do this. She had come this far. Then, after this last little bit, she would go to Ian. She had promised Mirinda she would. She had even promised to meet Mirinda for tea after this little tête-a-tête. Then she would tell all, feeling finally whole and useful, as she had not in years and years.

She smiled to herself and stopped just before Ballantine's shop window. Giving a pat to her cream straw hat and her cascade of light brown curls, she turned the knob and heard the ting-a-ling of his bell over her head.

"Good afternoon, Lady Murdoch!" Ballantine emerged from his back room, both hands extended. "How lovely you look today. But then, you look lovely every day I see you, milady."

"Thank you, Mr Ballantine. You are very kind."

"You are in the pink today, are you not?" he chuckled. "Literally and figuratively, I say! What a stunning walking suit."

"Thank you, sir. I did walk today. It is so lovely." She removed her gloves and put two fingers to her brow. "However," she sagged a little, "I wonder if you might . . . Oh, my. Yes, why thank you, Mr Ballantine. I do need your assistance. Might I sit, do you think? In that chair, over there?"

"Why, yes, of course, milady." He propped her up with one hand to her elbow, and when she began to melt once more, he hooked an arm round her waist.

"Oh, oh . . . my!" She sank into the monstrously uncomfortable chair with the wild springs. "Oh, oh . . . my," she shifted this way and that to avoid the daggers of its innards. "I say, Mr Ballantine, might I ask you for—"

"A cup of tea, milady? How's that? I was just making some in my office. I'd be happy to offer you a cup. Might help you revive, I think."

"Yes, thank you. I would love a cup of tea." She set her chatelaine on the tiny flower table to her left, her parasol to her right, and watched him go.

He moved off toward his back room, his girth oozing around the larger pieces of art very carefully.

She leaned forward and peered into the case. Yes. The ivory nail covers still sat amid the velvet.

"I wonder, Mr Ballantine," she called to him, coughing for effect, "if you might have a bit of honey for your tea?"

"What did you say, ma'am?" he yelled from his back room.

"Honey? Do you have any honey for your tea?"

He stuck his head out of his doorway. "No, ma'am. No honey. Just good black tea."

"Thank you," she smiled pleasantly at him, and he returned to his brewing.

Her eyes ran round the room in search of items Lee had itemized.

A calligrapher's set of pearl-encrusted brushes?

No.

A small translucent china ink cup, such as only Confucian *literati* or Manchu noblemen would use or could afford?

No.

A woman's matching vanity set of vermilion lacquered mirrors, combs and brushes, and perfume and ointment jars?

No.

Nothing else.

No, nothing else.

Panic rose in her chest. She grew short of breath and wondered if she could really see this through. What if . . .

No. She would not panic or flee. This was her mystery to solve. Hers to decipher.

Her eyes fell to the two ivory nail covers.

If this was indeed the only item Ballantine had, then she would discuss these, for heaven's sake. Just these.

He appeared at her side, smiling, holding a tea tray above his swelling middle. "Here we are, milady. Do you feel any better?"

Slowly, Clare. Slowly. "Only a fraction, I am sorry to say. I am certain a good cup of tea will do wonders for me."

He sank down opposite her in the chair he had occupied last Wednesday. With great efficiency, he poured steaming liquid into a yellow china cup and offered it to her. "I'm not much for pouring tea formally, ma'am. You understand."

She nodded. "I do, sir. Thank you." She reached for the sugar bowl and stirred in a spoonful, then took a sip. "Wonderful, Mr Ballantine, simply wonderful." She sat back in her chair.

"I have your pair of fu dogs for you, ma'am."

"Do you? Thank you. I am delighted you had a pair. Do you think I might trouble you to bring them out? I hate to interrupt your teatime, but I would like to see them before I purchase them."

"Certainly," is what he said but did not mean. In any case, he rose with difficulty from his chair and headed for his back room. The few moments gave

183

Clare time to breathe, time to plan—and she found she had done none of it when he once more stood before her.

"Here they are," he said as he placed them on the counter of a nearby table. What with the tea tray on the showcase in front of them, he could not have placed the two dogs there.

"Oh, they are lovely," Clare enthused over the two beautifully ugly bright red dogs.

"You do like them." He grinned. "I do myself. Nice wedding gift, too."

"Appropriate."

"Very."

They were coming to the end of their polite but forced conversation. Now it was her turn.

"May I have more tea, perhaps, Mr Ballantine?"

He eyed her but, like a good host, poured more tea into the cup she offered.

She suspected he knew she was prevaricating. Gad, where were her talents as an accomplished woman?

Clare cast him an engaging smile. "Thank you, sir." She sank down into the awful chair once more and twitched when the thing spiked her in a most unmentionable place. "The chair," she murmured.

He winced. "I do apologize, ma'am. I keep telling myself I must have it repaired. But . . . well, you know how costly things are these days."

"Yes," she sipped her tea, "I do indeed. I cannot imagine running a shop."

His eyes popped. "No, ma'am. You being from the aristocracy, I wouldn't think you could."

"I do wonder what it would be like, though to . . . well, you know, have a wonderful place to come to each morning." She arched her brows as if in invitation of his comment.

He fought a frown. "It is not as appealing as you might assume, ma'am."

"No?" She brightened and held out her cup for more tea.

"No," he said as he dribbled the remains of his tiny pot into her cup. "There is much work. Much worry."

"Why, Mr Ballantine, whatever should you worry over?"

"The quality. The customers demand quality, you know. And it is difficult to guarantee such things, particularly when supply is so limited. And so very difficult."

"Ah, yes. I see your point. And your problems. But I must tell you, every time I have been here, the quality and the quantity have delighted me."

He nodded his head, pleased.

"Take for example your current supply of goods." She emptied her cup and set it before him. "Yours was the only shop which had three pair of fu dogs. And these nail covers! Why, Mr Ballantine, I have never seen such a striking pair here in the West. The last time I saw anything comparable was in Shanghai more than twenty years ago."

"They are rare."

"Rare, yes. And I do adore them. Mr Ballantine, I wonder if you have any more hot water and tea leaves? I am so thirsty. I cannot imagine what's the matter with me. I am still recovering from an illness last winter. And I have *so* enjoyed your tea."

"Well, yes, ma'am." He rose, not happy about it but moving in any case.

She heard him fumbling in the back and she rose. Perhaps if she didn't have to face him, she could ask

185

the pertinent questions.

"I am intrigued by those nail covers, Mr Ballantine."

"Are you?" he called from the back, his voice very peeved.

"You say you bought them from a Chinese man, is that so?"

"Yes."

"Not long ago?"

"That's right."

"And he was young and spoke English brokenly?"

"Did I say that?"

"Yes. I wonder if you remember anything else about him?"

"Oh?" He was moving about, clinking china and kettle. "Such as what, milady?"

"If he had a queue?"

No sound came from the back of the room.

Clare stepped closer to the doorway and could not see him. "I say, Mr Ballantine, would you remember if the man had a queue?"

"No, ma'am," he said on the thread of a sound. "He had no queue."

Oh, God. Lo-wu had been here. He had sold the nail covers to Ballantine. It was true. Now, the only thing she had to know was if it was Ballantine who had killed him. But what to say? What to do?

Ballantine appeared in the doorway, a smile wreathing his face but wariness lining his brow. "Here is more tea, ma'am. Come back to the chair and sip it. I wouldn't want you going out without a bracer. I already put your sugar in it. Drink up."

She did. She knew she shouldn't, but there was no other way to avoid it. She sat, this time in the exact spot that had no wayward springs.

He poured tea.

She watched.

He offered it to her and she sipped. "Thank you. It is very good."

"I would say so, from the way you have thrown it down, ma'am."

"I do like the nail covers, you see."

"Do you really?" he asked, and she could have sworn he didn't believe a word she said.

"Yes, and I really would like to purchase them, but I do wonder about their authenticity. I have no need for anything which is not the very best."

"Hmm. Yes. And?" He sat back, one hand upon the armrest of his chair, eyeing her curiously.

"And I do wonder if a pair of nail covers *is* authentic if indeed the man had no queue. He might not be Chinese, you see, and —"

"He was Chinese, ma'am. I know them, I do."

"Well, yes, I would never dispute your knowledge of —"

"What then *are* you disputing, Lady Murdoch?"

"I —" She put a hand to her forehead as the room began to spin. "I think I —" She was going to be ill. Very ill.

He leaned forward, his bulging face seeming to blossom this close.

She noted his eyes. Blue. His nose. Red. And then, ever so politely, she closed her eyes to utter blackness.

Sixteen

What are you doing, Clare? Come along!

Mirinda paced the corner of Jermyn Street and Duke of York. She had been down the block to Piccadilly and back three times now, and still Clare had not emerged from the Ballantine Emporium. And Mirinda was not wrong: They *were* to meet here for tea. Clare had said half three. She had even suggested Willoughby's for tea. It was her favourite tearoom. Besides, to induce Clare to tell all with even greater rapidity, Mirinda had said *she* would pay the fare.

So where was Clare?

Mirinda, Mirinda, accept it. Clare is still in there. And she is having a bit of trouble, else she would have emerged long ago.

Mirinda made for the Ballantine Emporium with all the purpose of one of Her Majesty's Ships.

Opening the mauve stained-glass door to a little ting-a-ling, she looked about and saw no one.

"Good afternoon?" she called into the vacuum. "Hello-o?" She strode about, noting a few of the treasures Clare had described. "Mister Ballantine?"

"Oh, hello. Good afternoon!" gushed a portly man as he practically ran through his office door. He was wiping his hands and had obviously been exerting himself mightily. "May I help you, ma'am?"

"Yes. I do hope so. I am Lady Mirinda Clively and I have come in search of my sister. Has she left?"

"Oh, yes. Yes, indeed she did. Over an hour ago."

Mirinda gave him the quelling Howard stare, knowing Grandmother Howard would have been delighted with the results.

Ballantine perspired noticeably from his upper lip.

"An hour ago. I see." Clare had not planned to enter the shop before an hour ago. So where? . . .

Mirinda's eyes scanned the room, and in one swoop, she saw Clare's silver chatelaine perched atop a tiny table near some chairs. Her eyes slid back to the man's.

"Thank you very much, Mr Ballantine."

He nodded agreeably, a pained look on his face.

"Very well, thank you. My sister and I must have misunderstood each other concerning the time. Thank you."

She turned to the left so that once more she might gaze at the silver purse. Yes, by its rectangular shape, it could be none other than Clare's.

Mirinda hastened her departure out the door and down the street. Out of view of his shop, she took up her former spot at the end of Jermyn Street. "What do I do now?" she muttered to herself, and spun right into a pair of iron-sinewed arms.

"Oh, God! Gus! What are you doing here?"

He steadied her on her feet. "I ask you the same, Mirinda."

"I am trying to decide how I might best find Clare."

Gus raised his chin toward the Ballantine Emporium. "She is in there. From where you have just come."

"Why do you know this?"

189

He smiled, but it was sad and heartfelt. "My staff and I have been watching Mr Ballantine for quite some time."

"You and your staff? I see. How long is some time?"

"Five days."

"But why?"

"I think I must ask you many questions, too, my dear." He raised his blue eyes to a darkly clad gentleman in a wide-brimmed hat on the opposite corner and nodded once. "Come with me, *Liebchen*"—he took her arm—"and I will tell you my secrets if you tell me yours. And of course, Clare's."

"Really, Gus! This is extraordinary. I cannot simply go with you . . ."

"I have my carriage, milady. And if you are quiet and compliant—I know how difficult that is for you, my love, but if you are, we might manage to get into my carriage in broad daylight and have no one serve us up with the soup at their dinner table tonight."

"I do not understand what this has to do with Clare," she objected as she kept pace with him, more out of fear and curiosity than out of compliance.

"That is what I will tell you, if you then reveal to me Clare's secrets." He brought her to a large black covered landau and opened the door. "Get in quickly, before I lose my German temper, darling."

She ground her teeth but climbed up the step, ducking to go inside. He joined her, sitting opposite, his top hat immediately landing in his lap.

His sparkling eyes ran down the length of her sky-blue day gown. "You are dressed for tea. Formal tea. Were you meeting Clare?"

"Yes. How did you know?"

"When she went in, she looked as if she were going to formal tea. So unlike a woman merely shopping." His eyes bored into Mirinda's.

"You are right, Gus. She and I were meeting at half three. I knew she went in to speak with this shop-keeper, this Mr Ballantine, and I went in to see if she was still there."

"And he said she is not."

"Yes. How do you know, and more, *why?*"

Gus tapped the top of the carriage twice with his cane and the coachman tapped twice with his foot. In a moment, the driver led the horses out slowly into the street.

Mirinda balked. "Where are we going?"

"We are following Mr Ballantine, it would appear."

"No! Why? Clare is —"

"Clare is either in the shop or she is not. And since you did not see her, *Liebchen,* she is most likely in a very large, very heavy teak war chest, which the man has been hoisting all by himself for the last twenty minutes into his lorry in the back of his store. We were about to enter to inquire after Clare when you arrived to pace the street corner. I need to know if she is in that chest."

"No! How do you know?"

"Baron von Macht has observed Ballantine do this, *Liebchen.*"

"You are mad."

"Or Baron von Macht is."

She examined his features and knew that the black-eyed, ebony-haired, devilishly efficient Prussian Baron whom she had met the other evening would never make mistakes. "But I see you are certain."

"The good Baron never errs, *Liebchen.* It is why

Bismarck adores him, employs him, and I refine him."

"The Baron is retained by you to protect you, Gus. What is he doing spying on my sister?"

Gus folded his arms and gazed at her. "He was spying, as you call it, not on Clare, but on Mr Ballantine. You see, we have reason to believe that Mr Ballantine knows more about a certain diplomatic incident than many others. Do you remember Saturday evening at dinner when Charles Beaumont discussed an incident that occurred years ago at the Taku Forts?"

"Yes. A murder of a Chinese gentleman, wasn't it?"

"Yes. Mr Ballantine was in the Taku Forts at the time. He left soon afterward."

"You suspect he is the man you seek who murdered the Confucian official?"

"Baron von Macht says so, yes."

"And Clare walked into the middle of this."

"Yes. And now you must tell me why, *Liebchen*. Do not turn your nose up at me, my darling. I know Clare has not left the shop. I think you know why. Why?"

"She has followed a trail of murder herself. From our front door, the man in our park, to Ballantine."

Gus scowled. "I do not like this. Tell me how she concluded this Ballantine was involved."

Mirinda revealed every morsel of information Clare had imparted, even the last bits about her confrontation with a frightened Lee Davenport yesterday afternoon. When she finished her soliloquy, Gus just sat staring into nothingness.

"*Mein Gott!* I never thought anyone could escape the Forbidden City. It is guarded night and day. What a feat! Tzu Hsi must be frantic beyond reason to find the Tung-chih emperor's missing concubine. And a pregnant one at that. *Mein grosser Gott!* She will scour the earth until she finds her. And if she or her agents are not responsible for—what is his name? Lo-Wu?—Lo-Wu's death, when Tzu Hsi's agents hear of this murder in your park, she will be upon us in a moment."

"How could she not know? The newspapers have reported it."

"But only once."

"That is because the Yard reports nothing."

He harrumphed. "That is because the Yard has no clues. No weapon. No motive. No suspects."

"But you do, Gus."

He considered her hazel eyes a moment. "Yes. Ballantine seems to have been running a smuggling ring for years. His goods pop up in his shop here. But they also appear in another shop, a pawn shop, near the Seven Dials in Mercer Street."

"A pawn shop?" she mused. "A discreet place to hide goods."

"*Natürlich.* And we are drawn to him and his ring because we must stop this group from stealing more. But also we must present to the Chinese government good faith that we find and punish Westerners who commit crimes against the Chinese people. We must show we are ethical, even if Tzu Hsi retains the right to act the despot at every turn."

"A dilemma of international scope."

"Which could ruin us all, Westerner and Chinese alike, *Liebchen.*"

"Meanwhile, Clare stands in the middle." Mirinda clenched her hands and stared out the coach window. "I hope you have quite a few men."

"Would seven do, my love?"

"Seven?"

"Each, a superb physical specimen. Chosen by me personally for intelligence, stamina, and power."

"Plus wit and charm with the ladies, too, I would imagine."

He grinned. "One achieves one's objectives in many ways, milady."

"And where do you keep these supreme examples of Adam?"

He spread his hands wide. "My footmen, milady. Who else?"

Her brows shot to her hairline. "You must pay them handsomely."

"Each is well worth it. The Baron has seen to their training. What they did not learn from their mothers in grace, or their fathers in discipline, or their universities in scholarship and statesmanship, he has instilled with rigour and finesse."

"Hmm. I must pay more attention to the noble Baron. He seems a paragon of all the virtues."

"He is incomparable, *Liebchen*. I rely on him totally and he has never failed me. He will not in this, either."

The carriage rolled to a stop and the coachman opened the door. The redoubtable Baron von Macht ducked inside to sit next to Gus. In one swift movement, he swept off his wide-brimmed hat and ran a quick hand through his black-as-midnight hair. He nodded to Mirinda in greeting and looked at Gus.

"*Mein Prinz,* we are at the front entrance to Ballantine's factory along the Thames. He has arrived and is dragging the war chest inside. We have options."

"Describe the one you favour, *mein Herr.*"

The Baron's onyx eyes skidded to Mirinda and back. "We wait."

Gus moved not a muscle.

The Baron understood. "We are eight. Ballantine may have more than that number inside. Not knowing our opponent's size and condition, I would not suggest attack until our *Soldaten* estimate the situation and/or insinuate themselves into their territory."

Mirinda thought the Baron sounded exactly like a general arranging his soldiers.

Gus considered that a moment. "You have ten minutes to accomplish your reconnaissance, Baron. You are armed?"

Mirinda shivered.

The Baron blinked not a lash. *"Jawohl, mein Prinz."*

Gus nodded. The interview was ended.

The Baron inclined his head to Mirinda and backed out the way he'd come in.

Ten minutes passed in dead silence.

The coachman opened the door and Gus alighted first, giving his hand up to assist Mirinda. The imposing Baron stood rigidly before them, his eyes trained over Gus's shoulder.

"Mein Prinz, we go in. No one is inside but Ballantine and, obviously, Lady Murdoch."

"Go." Gus took Mirinda's elbow to lead her in a leisurely pace over the graveled courtyard. "We follow."

"But—" She pointed to Baron von Macht who hastened off.

"We *follow*. We allow the Baron to do his duty, *Liebchen.*"

Mirinda swallowed, her mouth trembling as she

fought back tears.

He squeezed her elbow. "You must learn to trust the Baron as I do, my love. He will rescue Clare. Never doubt."

They walked down the courtyard to stand before the front entrance to a three-story red brick factory which must have been built centuries before. Broken bricks dotted the courtyard and the scruffy tufts of grass. Shards of glass from gaping windows scattered upon the uneven pavement. Even the double front doors, which were twice the size of a man's width, needed a good coat of paint.

They stepped onto the walkway leading to the front door, and one burly blond man emerged from behind an untamed boxwood where he had been hiding. He strode before them, his head constantly swiveling from left to right. Their guard dog, Mirinda concluded.

Indeed, he thrust open the double doors, his large, nasty-looking handgun before him. He waved them both in, and they entered a gloomy, musty, empty warehouse. Somewhere below them, the sound of scuffling made Mirinda turn to Gus with fear.

"Mein Prinz?"

It was the Baron's voice emerging through the floorboards.

Their Cerberus turned to them, his electric blue eyes acknowledging that Gus and she might respond.

Footsteps ran toward them. From a flight of stairs at the rear, Baron von Macht appeared, wild-eyed.

"Mein Prinz, bitte. Kommen Sie mit mir."

"Was ist los, Baron?"

Black eyes slid to Mirinda. *"Ballantine ist tot."*

Gus circled his arm around Mirinda's waist.

"Dead!" She sagged in horror. "How?"

"Garotted, *mein Prinz*."

"And Lady Murdoch?"

"She is not here."

"Not?! . . ." Gus shook with the fury of Thor. *"Gott im Himmel!* What the hell do you mean, von Macht? Where in Christ is she, then?"

The Baron never so much as breathed. "The teak war chest is gone, sir. Please, come see for yourself."

Gus clutched Mirinda to his side, and in his blue outrage, she would have sworn she felt his blood pump through his massive veins. If he crushed her in his anger, he would never know. His temper was notorious—to her, to Bismarck, to his wife, his sisters—and he knew and contained it at most times. But his anger numbed her and she felt him rage on at his man, while the terror of what had happened to Clare loomed like a living hell.

She broke free and made for the stairs.

"Mirinda!"

"I must see," she shot back to him, and she could hear how he left off reprimanding the Baron and followed her.

"Mirinda, for Christsakes," he muttered as he came up behind her, running down the dusty stairs at a fast clip. "Wait. You have no need to see a man who's been garotted!"

"I don't care about Ballantine. I must find Clare!"

She came to a halt at the bottom of the stairs, and the dust-moated gloom Mirinda made out six figures standing in a circle. At their feet was a body.

She picked up her skirts and moved closer.

Eyes open, mouth agape, hands wide, legs askew, Ballantine had met his Maker.

197

She turned away and into Gus's waiting arms.

"Does the Baron have any clue to where Clare might be?" she asked of Gus, her words muffled by his large wool lapels and red silk cravat.

Gus stroked her hair as, in German, he asked his chagrined Baron what he knew. The Baron strode off with six of his men, leaving the tall blond Cerberus with Gus and Mirinda. Within minutes, the group returned.

"Mein Prinz," Baron von Macht said in a mournful voice, "we think we know what happened to Lady Murdoch."

Mirinda did not need to look at the man to hear the trepidation in his voice.

"We have looked everywhere in this building. It is an old supply building for munitions, we think, and has numerous tunnels and drop chutes to the river. We have found one chute, recently used. Very recently used, within minutes, I would say, because we have found these items." He handed over a small copper coin and a piece of parchment to Gus. "They were beside the open hatch."

Gus glanced at the coin and pocketed it. Then he flicked open the folded note with a twist of his fingers. His eyes went blank.

"Gus?" Mirinda grabbed his arm. "What is it? Not ransom?"

"Not ransom," he said dazedly. "A note I know well." His sad eyes met hers squarely. "Because I wrote it."

"What?"

"Mirinda, I understand only that whoever has been here, I know."

"But . . . that doesn't . . . Oh, God. I have learned

198

that *anything* can make sense. I have learned that. But, please, where is Clare?"

Baron von Macht shrank in his suit. "Lady Clively, I wish I could say. But the open chute where we found that note is used to send cargo down swiftly to the riverbank. From what we determine, the teak war chest has been sent down this chute into the Thames."

Gus scowled. "And where is it now, Baron?"

"Mein Prinz, we cannot see any chest from the factory dock above the chute's exit from the building. Therefore, we do not know where the chest has gone."

Gus cursed in ribald German. "Meaning what, Baron?"

"We do not know if it has floated downriver or if— forgive me, Lady Clively—it has sunk to the bottom of the river."

Seventeen

Clare accepted the proffered hand of the fish coster and slid from the lorry seat to the cobbled street in front of Clively Close.

"Thank you very much, sir. I do appreciate your help so much. I do not know what I would have done without your kindness, and I would like to give you a small token of my gratitude. If you would be so good as to come with me to the door, I—"

"Ah, no, mum," the almost-toothless, tiny man shook his bald head. "Thank ye kindly, I do. But I don' think I can take payment for being a good Samaritan, mum."

He eyed the lovely lady in the crumpled rose linen. Aye. A lady, she was. But a bit daft, if you asked him. Talk of sailin' down the Thames in a box, bumpin' the banks, and rollin' onto the green well south o' Tower Bridge. She had a few ticks in the noggin, all right. But he'd figured he'd humour her. Hell, he needed a few good deeds on his ledger. The Reverend Woodley would like the tale, for fair.

"If you're sure?"

"Aye, mum." He glanced about at the pretty new townhouses, anxious to be gone from this part o' town where he never went, only his fancier fish. He twirled his Irish cap between two hands. "I think I'll be on me way."

Clare watched him round his red truck, stick his hat on his shiny pink head, and take up the reins of his old brown and white sorrel. Well, he wouldn't take money, but she could do other things for him. Yes, she could and she would. "Peter's Fish and Such" said the peeling gold lettering on the faded red enamel.

"Easy to remember," she mused aloud as she waved him off. "Like Peter, the Lord's Fisherman. From this day forward, we shall order our fish from Peter the Fisherman."

She smiled, then grabbed her stomach as the lorry moved off, trailing an aroma that was decidedly fishy.

She felt decidedly sick. Ugh. She turned slowly and gazed at Scarborough House. Its lovely hulking shape brought tears to her eyes. Thank God. Home.

She had thought never to see it again. Never.

Perhaps if she could just make it to the Clively bench and sit and enjoy the lovely summer air, she would feel more like her old self. Oh, God. She started for the bench, each step a challenge to her will and her wobbly legs. Weak episodes made her wonder if she would ever recover her strength, her once-robust good health.

At least this time, she knew the spell was caused by something other than the horrible malady she had suffered all winter.

Gad, if the cold didn't kill you, your art dealer would try.

She stumbled across the grass and sank onto the blessed bench. One elbow to the back of the bench, one hand to her forehead, she told herself to breathe evenly, deeply, serenely. She had to recover. She had to! For the first time in years—actually, since Ian had grown and left her care to join his father's Black Watch regiment—she had a purpose, a reason to her life. She was assisting a friend in dire circumstances. She would not lose her life doing it. She would *not!*

She glanced up at her father and considered the man. He had fought in battles. God, he'd faced death over and over! But she had only prim, proper Victorian London in which to survive. If Clarence Clively could face the terrors of bayonets and rifles and mortar, by God, she could survive this wicked chest infection . . .

Clare inhaled and the warm summer breeze filled her senses. She might survive Victorian London, but what of surviving men such as Ballantine? Or had, indeed, Ballantine himself survived?

She was not sure.

Not sure at all.

Something about what had happened while she was in that terrible box danced at the edges of her memory.

She rubbed her eyes. Her vision was still blurry. Her head still ached. The sun was setting, so it was probably hours since premature darkness had descended on her in Ballantine's shop. Hours since she had drunk his tea—and whatever he had slipped into it. Hours since she was to meet Mirinda with news of her little investigation.

Little investigation? Ha! What a misnomer. What an error! How could she have been so naive?

She shrugged and nodded to herself. She knew how. She was a Victorian lady, with all the inbred propriety, all the social doctrine drilled into her. She still possessed all the normal assumptions that people were honest, upright, caring, and moral. The mystery of the murdered baby in the chimney should have taught her that evil lurks in the heart and mind of anyone. Yes, provided one had enough motivation to overturn the "normal assumptions" and grind them to useless dust, anyone was capable of any dastardly deed.

The deed Ballantine had committed, though, eluded her. Oh, certainly, he had drugged her. Of that, she had no doubt. Drugged her and dragged her and put her in that hideous teak chest.

Ooh. She shivered, remembering the cobwebs she had picked from her brilliant if dirt-smudged rose suit as she stood on the riverbank contemplating a part of London — if indeed it still was London — that she did not know. She was positive she had never seen the place, whatever it was.

But she had not stood about fretting. Immediately, she had climbed the grassy knoll on hands and knees, landing smack in the middle of a major thoroughfare. She must have looked dazed, crazed . . . Gad, no hat, no chatelaine, no parasol, and worst of all, no gloves! Totally undressed, she was.

Yet, the first conveyance she saw, she waved down. Peter the Fisherman, God bless his soul, took pity on her and pulled his lorry to a halt at her feet. Then he had brought her home, his eyes lingering on every Bobby he saw along the way lest he need help to restrain her if she broke out in song, breast-beating, or a little jig.

And of course, she had done none of that.

A huge black landau rattled to a stop at the foot of the Clively Circle. Stopped, discharged a few passengers, and then started again at the driver's response to some order from inside.

Clare told herself she really should not sit out here any longer. She felt better, thanks to the gentle sunshine and air. And her head did not pound so furiously.

"Clare?" Mirinda was running through the park, Gus close on her heels. "My God! Clare!" Indy sank down before Clare, her hazel eyes all over each inch of her body. "Where have you been? We've been searching everywhere!"

Gus stood behind Indy, scowling like a blond angel. "Please, Clare, tell us."

A tall, dark man in total black came to stand at Gus's right. If Gus were God's angel, this marvelous specimen was the hellishly beautiful assistant of the Fallen Angel. Yet, he said nothing. Only his black eyes spoke of fright and relief.

"I just arrived, actually. Got a ride home with a fish coster. Peter the Fisherman. We must remember to tell Pence to buy our fish from him, Indy. He brought me here straightaway and would not—"

"Clare, for heaven's sake," Indy had tears in her eyes now. "Stop rattling on, will you, and tell us where you were before Peter the Wolf—"

"Peter the *Fisherman*."

"*Who*ever he was! How did you meet Peter?"

"Oh, quite by accident, I assure you."

By the quelling Howard look in her eye, Indy was going to carve Clare up for haggis, certainly. But Gus and his friend stepped forward.

"Baron von Macht and I will assist you, Clare. You do not appear fully recovered." Gus took one arm and his Baron the other. As she walked, she enjoyed the assistance so much—and needed it so badly—Clare did wonder how she had gained the Clively bench without any help at all. The excitement, she told herself. That's what it must have been.

Safely inside her parlour, Clare watched stoically as half a dozen people seemed in perpetual motion. Indy was giving orders for tea, brandy, hot packs, and lavender-scented towels to a wide-eyed Hopkins. Gus was plumping pillows for her. The enigmatic Baron von Macht was fetching a footstool and removing her soggy shoes to massage her feet. Colette stood in one corner, calm but frowning at the Baron. Meanwhile, Patsie, who had been dusting in the hallway when the party had come in, gaped at them all.

Clare felt the imp emerge from her secret depths. It felt rather lovely to have so many concerned about her. It felt even more divine to have this man administering to her feet, of all things! Her eyes drifted from his long, strong, slim fingers wrapped around her silk-stockinged ankle and toes, sliding up his black-clad torso and white linen shirt to his chiseled jaw, sharp cheeks, arched brows, and heavy shock of ebony hair, once precisely combed and now hanging over his fathomless black eyes.

"This helps, *ja?*"

"*Ja.*" *I could develop an addiction to such ministrations.* "*Dankeschön, Baron.*"

"*Bitte,* Lady Murdoch, my name is Stefan."

Stefan? Stefan of the mesmerizing eyes, aristocratic nose, and ruddy complexion. Stefan of the expressive hands. Stefan, all of thirty-two or thirty-three? Well, she was not so ill that she missed the importance of him giving her his first name. Against propriety, he was to be called Stefan.

"I must apologize to you, Lady Murdoch."

"*Bitte,* Stefan, my name is Clare. Why must you apologize to me, sir?"

"I was responsible for your health and welfare, and I failed to insure it."

She laughed a little. "I am afraid, Stefan, I am either still in a muddle or innately thick in the head, but I have no idea what you are trying to convey."

He continued his task with long, sure strokes to the bottom of her feet. "I was given the task of surveying your entry and egress from the Ballantine Emporium, and it was I who said we should inspect the factory where you were taken before we entered. By waiting, I allowed Ballantine the opportunity to send you down the river."

Stefan's head bent so that Clare saw only his glossy black hair and felt only her fingers tingle with the urge to rake it.

"Forgive me, Clare. I lost you."

"I am very afraid I still do not know what you are talking about."

Gus drew near.

"Baron von Macht has, shall we say, certain responsibilities to me in my employ, Clare. One of them is to assist me in investigating matters on which I require enlightenment."

"Why, Gus, do you need enlightenment about Mr Ballantine?"

Mirinda, who had shooed Patsie and Colette out the parlour door, came to sit opposite Clare in a grandiose Queen Anne chair. She took her sister's hand. "It seems, my dear, that Gus has suspected Mr Ballantine of certain criminal actions which have a bearing on Chinese politics."

Clare's mind cleared as if doused with cold water. "I understand the relevance instantly, but not the logic. Someone please explain to me."

Gus sighed and strode to the fireplace. One elbow to the mantel, one forefinger aside his mouth, he stared into the dead hole. "Mr Ballantine has been importing various goods from Chinese ports for many years. Twenty-two years, to be precise. In one of his ventures a few years ago, he was near the scene of a rather ugly murder."

Gus turned to face Clare. "In this incident, a Confucian scholar was murdered, his body stripped of all his goods. The murder occurred on Chinese soil, not in a Treaty Port."

"Ahh," said Clare. "Therefore, the Chinese government demanded the criminal be turned over to them for trial and punishment."

"Exactly," said Gus. "The Europeans have extraterritorial rights to prosecute their own nationals only in their own Treaty Ports. But this murder occurred just outside the boundaries of the Taku

Forts, and therefore, Tzu Hsi demands the barbarians produce the culprit."

"Meanwhile, we barbarians have had no clues as to his identity."

"Correct. Or very few clues."

"What new evidence do you have now, Gus?"

"One of the items taken from the dead man was something very rare. Very indicative of his rank and prestige."

How did she know what the item was? Why did she have to ask? "A pair of ivory nail covers."

Gus simply stared into her eyes.

"How did you know they were there, Gus?"

Stefan stopped stroking Clare's feet to gaze at her. "I went into the Emporium last week and saw them in the display case. I knew immediately we had found something important."

Gus rose on his toes and clasped his hands behind him. "Now, of course, we find these same nail covers are important to you in your investigation of the murder of the man in the park. We must hear your logic, Clare. I confess, I am confused, even with Mirinda's explanation."

"It is really quite simple. When I was in last week looking for fu dogs for a wedding present for Julia and Dominik, I spied these in the case. They are quite extraordinary, you know."

Gus nodded and Stefan inclined his head in agreement.

Hopkins knocked once, then opened the doors to creep in with a huge tea tray. Mirinda motioned for him to set it upon Clare's large reading table in the corner and began to pour as Hopkins disappeared through the door.

"I saw them and had to know where they had come from. How he had acquired them. I thought he had gotten them here in England, and with this murder of the man in the park on my mind, I asked him if he had purchased them from a Chinese. Ballantine said he did. He even said the man spoke some English. Pidgin English. I drew the conclusion, which may now be totally incorrect, that it was our man from the park, Lo-wu, who had sold them to him."

Mirinda placed a steaming cup of black pekoe in Clare's hands. "Thank you, my dear. Then when I told Lee Davenport yesterday afternoon what I suspected about Yi-an's true identity and Lo-wu's actions, she told me Lo-wu had brought with him out of China some of his family treasures. His plan was to sell the treasures to fund his and Yi-an's life together. But, of course," she swallowed some of her tea with tearful difficulty, "that is not to be."

Gus shook his head. "And did Lee Davenport describe Lo-wu's nail covers?"

"Yes, Gus. She simply said they were three-inch-long ivories."

Gus looked at the Baron. "How certain can we be that the nail covers in Ballantine's are the ones stolen and not from this Bannerman Lo-wu's collection?"

"We—*I* am certain, *mein Prinz*. The design of the phoenix is given only to government officials of the highest rank by the Dragon Throne. This official had the phoenix. The nail covers in the Emporium bear the phoenix. I have made no mistake on this."

"Sehr gut, mein Herr." Gus leveled his copen blue gaze once more at Clare. "We are assured, then, that we have established Ballantine's complicity in the Chinese official's murder in the Taku Forts two years ago. We may assume, then, that your inquiries about the nail covers made him nervous about your interest and that he tried to silence you for that interest."

"Yes, but there are problems in that logic. If he did acquire the nail covers in the Taku Forts and openly offer them for sale, he did not fear discovery here in England. If however he acquired the nail covers from a young Chinese man here in England, then there would be no need to fear what I knew."

Mirinda shook her head. "Unless, somehow, he knew about Lo-wu's nail covers and feared you would connect him to Lo-wu's murder."

"Or he knows who did kill Lo-wu, and sought to drug me and do away with me because I would be a threat." Somehow that rankled less than the insult to her intelligence, her sleuthing ability. "Ha! When I think of how easy it was to drug me, I cringe at my naivete!"

Mirinda sprang from her chair. "Drug you?"

"Yes. Indy, you can rest assured I did not step into that war chest on my own. But I did ask for tea, God help me. So, as Ballantine's and my conversation progressed, and my questions continued, it was ever so simple for Ballantine to retreat to his office, brew me more tea, slip in something—I'd guess it was laudanum from the headache I have—and do with me what he willed."

The Baron bristled, his hands gripping her toes.

"Clare, what did the man do?"

She had to chuckle, but when everyone else looked rather funereal, she stopped. "Nothing except, I would gather, to put me in that hideous teak war chest. Dirty thing it was, too." She picked at her once-delectable rose walking suit.

"A wonder the thing didn't sink," said Mirinda.

"That's what we thought," said Gus.

"I had my men scour the riverbank," murmured Stefan. "I thought I had lost you. I blame myself. I promise you, Clare, I shall protect you from now on with all diligence." His eyes shot to Gus. "Do I have your permission, *mein Prinz,* to post a guard here?"

"Jawohl, Baron."

Stefan took one of Clare's hands and enfolded it between his own two. "No one will hurt you anymore."

"Thank you, Stefan, but I really do not think *I* need protection." She looked at Gus, and in the space of a few moments, she saw what she had not actually seen in the factory. The "vision" danced before her eyes. Her mind whirled, her nostrils flared, and she was up and out of her chair, walking toward the window that looked out over the garden. She remembered something elusive, ever elusive.

"I do not need protection because—" she gained on the three, "Ballantine is dead, isn't he?"

"Yes," said Mirinda. "How do you know?"

"Because I heard him die. Strangulation, unless I miss my guess."

Stefan was out of his chair, coming toward her.

211

"Do you mean to say he died *before* the chest was sent down the chute?"

Chute, eh? So she had not dreamt of flying, just as she had not dreamt of sailing. Gad. She really *had* done both today.

"Yes, Stefan. I think the person who did in Mr Ballantine meant to free me."

Stefan ran both hands through his hair. "Explain that to me, please, Clare."

"He—my savior was a man, from the sound of his gruff voice—he was very angry with Ballantine for his actions against me. Said Ballantine had overreacted. Cursed him roundly, too."

Mirinda clutched her throat. "Could you identify this man's voice?"

"Was he British?" asked Gus.

Clare stared at her sister, remembering. "He spoke perfect English."

"You are certain?" prompted Gus.

Clare ran both hands over her eyes. She was losing the vision, the feeling, as quickly as it had come. "Oh, God, I am not sure. I was drifting in and out of the drug's euphoria. Awful stuff, laudanum."

"Yes, it is," said Mirinda as she looped an arm around Clare's shoulders and steered her back to her chair.

"Perhaps Clare is correct," mused Stefan. "The chute the trunk went down was one with more of a landing at its base than the others. Perhaps the man who freed her did mean to save her."

"If that is true, *mein Herr,*" said Gus, "then the man who killed Ballantine knows this factory very well. After all, he acted so quickly, he not only deposited Clare appropriately, he also escaped our men easily."

"Ja, das ist richtig, mein Prinz."

"Listen to me, Baron," said Gus between his teeth. "I care not for being right on a flimsy stretch of logic. I care only to be right on solid logic."

"Ich verstehe, mein Prinz. I not only understand, I agree. More than that, I wish to establish the truth, once and for all."

"Then make sure it is done, Baron, with all due haste."

The Baron bowed. "I will send two men back to the factory building to investigate for any little thing we may have missed. Also, I will set up a guard of four men here, twenty-four hours a day."

Clare shook her head. "I think I am safe. Ballantine is dead. And I was freed. Obviously, the murder in the Taku Forts and the murder in the park are not related, else I would have died. I think the person who needs protection more is Lee Davenport."

Gus frowned. "I really am confused at your logic, Clare."

"If Ballantine did not kill Lo-wu, someone else did. Most likely an agent of Tzu Hsi. Lee refuses to leave and cannot with Yi-an in poor health. The police do not see a connection and will not post a guard. In fact, if they did, such attention might draw the Empress's agent to Lee's door. We could not chance it. Only you can protect them, Gus. You and the Baron and your men."

Gus jammed his hands in his trouser pockets and

213

turned to contemplate the dark fireplace again. "I will post the guard here and at Mrs Davenport's. See that it is done, Baron."

"But, Gus," said Clare, "I have just explained I do not need protection!"

"Yes, you do, Clare," Gus whispered, then turned back to them all. "Yes, you do."

He extracted a slip of paper from his pocket and unfolded it, extending it for all to see.

"This note was found on the floor near the chute."

Mirinda, Stefan, and Clare shook their heads, not understanding Gus's implication.

"Whoever sent you on your way, Clare, is a very intelligent person. And also very careless. This note proves it."

Clare raised a brow. "What is it?"

"A schedule of meetings in the Foreign Office."

"So whoever freed me works for Her Majesty's government?"

"No, Clare. To be precise, whoever sent you to the riverbank works with me."

"What?!"

"I wrote this note."

"You?"

"I wrote it this morning in my own hand at my desk and dispersed it personally to my cohorts on my special committee. Sad to say, whoever sent you down that chute works with me. And I must find him before he murders anyone else."

Eighteen

A screeching sound made Clare bolt upright in bed.

Who was that?

What was that?

Reality or her nightmare?

She rubbed her eyes and reached for the warm emerald robe with the French lace collar. Dragging her unbraided, unbound hair from beneath the dressing robe, she put on her slippers and headed for the stairs.

It was some dark time of the night and the gas flames burned low in the wall sconces. She went down the stairs easily, quickly, more quickly than her pounding heart told her was wise.

On the main floor, no one was about.

Who could be? Who would be? The Baron von Macht and three of his men were posted round the house.

But where were they? She had retired long before the specifics were decided. The adventures of the day had sent her to bed with a headache that only a lavender-scented compress could cure.

But what was that noise?

She flung open the door to her parlour and

scanned the room. No one was about.

She opened her dining room door and found no one there, either.

Not in the butler's pantry.

Nor her drawing room.

The conservatory?

She flung open the door to find Baron von Macht, arms akimbo, frowning at her accursed parrot.

"Stefan? What seems to be the matter?"

He turned calmly but fury was written on his features as his appreciative eyes swept her figure. "Clare, how wonderful . . . This bird speaks German."

"Yes. I know," she said, closing the door and walking forward to stare at the imperturbable beast in the cage.

"Very *bad* German," he elaborated.

"Really?"

"He needs a proper education."

Clare chuckled. "Oh, no, Stefan, please! Do not teach this animal anything else. He is outrageous as it is!"

"I know. I was sitting here with your sister, and at my German exclamation of *mein Gott,* the thing went mad!"

"He is prone to that. Quiet as a titmouse, dead as a rat, until something sparks his insane desire to talk and talk and talk. I have never heard so much blather."

"Blather! Blather!" The bird squawked and flapped his wings, hopping about his wire cage like one half his size.

Clare leaned forward and clucked at him. "Do be

quiet, you silly thing. You woke me up!"

"Woke me up! Woke me up!"

In disgust, Clare turned away from the bird just as Mirinda was coming through her conservatory door, Hopkins trailing behind with a huge tea tray.

"You're awake, Clare?" her sister asked, grinning and pleased.

"You woke me up!" yelled the bird. "You woke me up!"

"Hopkins?" began Clare.

"Yes, mum. I know, mum. Take the bird way, mum." He set down his tray, nodded to Mirinda, and headed for the parrot.

Mirinda positioned herself on the settee and began to pour. "Shall I pour a cup for you, too, my dear? The Baron and I were ripe for a little. Are you feeling better?"

"Yes, very much better, thank you." Clare took a seat opposite Indy while the Baron chose the chair nearest Clare. "I heard something—the bird, I suppose—and could not rest."

"Not another of your dreams?" Indy asked, her hazel eyes really asking if Clare had had any more *voyants*.

"Yes," Clare said slowly, accepting her tea, "I think so."

Stefan frowned. "You suffer from vivid dreams, Clare?"

"Yes, occasionally," she tried to sound nonchalant.

"My mother did, too. In reality," he said as he took his cup from Mirinda and sipped, "she had visions."

"Is that so?" Clare asked, feigning politeness.

"Yes. Very vivid visions. She could see scenes of occurrences in other sections of Berlin."

Clare paused.

Mirinda stopped pouring her own tea to examine the handsome Baron. A glance at Clare, then she asked him, "What kind of occurrences?"

"Once, a wedding. Her cousin who months later married a rich *Junker*. Another time, she saw a baby's birth. The son of my uncle. Once, she even foresaw a murder."

Clare almost dropped her china.

Mirinda was more composed. "How could that be?"

The Baron shrugged. "We never knew. Our priest said she must have been given special sight by God. Whoever it was who gave her such abilities, she never questioned. She simply accepted the gift and used it for good where and when she could."

Clare gulped down the last sip of tea. "I—I certainly cannot say I have powers equal to that. I cannot foretell, you see."

"Neither could she in the beginning. And it was only after she was older that she recognized the potential and began to develop it."

"Oh?" Clare stared at him. *That was interesting.*

"Yes, she claimed she did not have the acuity to deal with it when she was young. So anything she 'saw' she tended to dismiss. But later, when she was more serene, she could process the visions into something more meaningful." The Baron laughed, a fluid sound soothing to the tension Clare felt in her stomach. "Older was wiser and more courageous, she claimed."

"Yes," Clare murmured, "I see what she meant."

He placed his cup and saucer on the octagonal tea table and sat forward. "Clare, is there anything you see which you have not told us?"

She shook her head. "No. Gus and you know everything. I, very much like your mother, blotted out what I saw because I would not believe the incredible nature of what I knew to be true. I knew, you see, that the young woman was more than a cousin of Lee Davenport's. I knew from her shoes, her manner, her tone. I knew the murdered man in the park was a gentleman, but for lack of a more exact characterization, I could not say what kind of Chinese gentleman. Only the yellow banner gave me the clue. That and his lack of a queue." She inhaled and let her eyes meet the Baron's soft, dark ones. "What I failed to fully explore in my own mind was why a man would be castrated."

She came to at the forthrightness of the subject. "Forgive me, I forgot myself."

"No, Clare," said the Baron. "Continue, please."

"If I had explored that, perhaps I would have seen that to a Western man castration seems to be a suitable punishment for someone who has touched the Chinese emperor's concubine. After all, more than four thousand eunuchs tend the Chinese imperial family in Peking. And most of them serve the emperor's concubines because no real man may ever touch an emperor's mate. I fear the murderer of Lowu knew who he was, why he was here, and with whom."

She sighed. "Rest assured that from this day on, I will attempt to note every aspect, every minute detail in my visions, so that I might understand them more quickly and more fully." She put her teacup down. "If I had done that sooner, perhaps Mr Ballantine would not be dead."

Mirinda tisked. "Now, Clare, do not assume guilt in that man's death! *He* tried to kill you, do not forget."

"I know, but somehow I think if I had analyzed my visions more fully, he would not have tried to hurt me."

"Nein! Das ist nicht richtig, meine Frau. He would have tried. Remember, I have proof he was present at the murder of the Chinese official in Taku two years ago."

"What kind of proof?" Clare asked. "The nail covers could only mean he obtained them from someone who knew the dead man, not—"

The Baron held up a hand. *"Bitte.* One man will swear to Ballantine leaving the official's house, running from the house just before the murdered man's body was found."

"That still does not prove Ballantine killed the official," she said.

"No. But his bloody knife does. Yes, it was Ballantine's knife which killed the man. Found after a search of the dead man's house. Found in the garden, along the path Ballantine took to escape the scene of the crime."

"If Ballantine did not kill the man himself, he knew who did," Clare affirmed.

"And now," mourned Mirinda, "that man is in London."

"Ja. And works with Prince Hessebogen on this commission."

A frisson of palpable fear made Clare close her eyes.

"And he let me go because—because he knew me."

They were all silent at that.

The Baron rose, heels together, bowing. "It is late, miladies, and I must consult with my men. I speak for them when I thank you, Lady Clively, for your assistance this evening with accommodations in the house. Thank you for the tea, too. And to you, Clare, I hope you recover quickly. Sleep well, both of you. Good evening." He nodded and was gone.

Mirinda sat, one finger tapping her cheek. "Doesn't it strike you as rather odd that a man of such grace and decorum and learning as the Baron addresses me as Lady Clively and you as Clare?"

Clare blushed and spread her hands wide in exclamation. "I have no explanation."

"What did you do to the poor fellow?"

Glee made Clare grin. "I swear I did nothing!"

"Except?"

"Nothing!"

Indy tilted her head to one side. "Are you changing like the Baron's mother, perhaps? Becoming, blossoming, beguiling men in your advanced years?"

Clare broke out laughing. "Look at me!" She picked at the way the dressing robe fell flat to her chest. "I am hardly the woman I used to be!"

Mirinda's eyes roved over her twin. "I should say so! Your complexion is pink again. Your hair is lustrous once more. You may still need to have Colette trim the gussets in your bosom, but you are different, Clare. You have bloomed with this investigation. And it is noticeable and attractive to men.

Do not ignore it. It is true." She giggled. "And interesting."

"Well, I shall tell you, my dear chuckling sister, that I am not interested."

"Aren't you?"

"Well, not in anything permanent. Only in a little casual—"

"Flirting."

"No!"

"That is what it is, my dear aghast sister. And what's the harm, I say, if you're fully set on flirting for flirting's sake?"

"I have other things to do besides flirt, Indy. I—I must attend to my visions. If I am to take Stefan's mother's course, I must begin to pay attention to them more. I must make myself more open to my own knowledge, as I have never done before. Gad, if I had done that, I wouldn't have to hide all these facts from Ian, and Gus wouldn't ask me to wait, either, because . . . just think, we might already know who the murderer of Lo-wu was! Or Ballantine's. We might know who of our acquaintances— and who of Gus's colleagues—had done this awful deed."

Mirinda was suddenly grave. "We cannot stew in this."

Clare knew the look, the tone, the gleam in her twin's eye. It spelled adventure. "What do you propose?"

Indy winked at Clare. "A few good ways to stir your senses."

Clare pulled her chin in to her neck. "Now, Indy. I have no need of men when—"

"Not men, my dear. We are going to a place

where you might stimulate your senses without public censor."

"And where might that be?"

"More tea, dear, before you turn in? No. Well! I have the perfect place, I do. Now, now, you will love it. We shall do a small bit of the British Museum tomorrow. Just a floor or two. A little Greek sculpture, a little Holbein, some terrifying El Greco from the Inquisition, and you should begin to stir!"

"Gad, Indy. If I look at that mélange in one afternoon, I will run from the place in a trance!"

Mirinda clasped her hands together and pursed her lips. "Nothing better, my dear."

Nineteen

Clare considered the pasty complexion of his fourth wife, Anne of Cleves, and had no doubts why Henry VIII of England had turned her out in favour of Catherine Howard. Catherine, distant ancestral relative of their own Grandmother Howard, had proven no finer a wife than a few of Henry's previous ones, and she was soon gone, too.

Clare turned for the sturdy bench in the center of the vaulted gallery and spread the glories of her new moss-green tucked laveuse skirt. Where was Indy?

Gone to see the little section housing a few Delacroixes and those other newer French painters whose works she liked so well. Leaving her with the burly blond Cerberus from Gus's and Stefan's pack walking about the room.

Clare really did not mind the wait. This had been a marvelous idea of Mirinda's. Marvelous.

Aside from the afternoon at The Henworth with John last week, she had not been out in so long—too long—and the confinement was wearing on her. Badly.

Perhaps she was coming out, as Indy said. Blossoming.

She giggled and clamped a hand over her mouth

224

when a passerby scowled at her.

Men. Well, frankly, she rather liked the whole idea. Not that any of them matched Robert. No, not ever. But she could enjoy them, couldn't she? She could enjoy their company, their conversation, their dramas. Certainly.

Just the way old Henry had enjoyed all his wives.

And if the exposure heightened her awareness of the world, politics, society . . . oh, who was she kidding?

She just wanted a little *fun*.

Her eyes traveled up another wall, landing on Henry himself. *You can not tell me, old man, you did not have any fun with all these women!* Well, a woman didn't have to sleep with a man to enjoy him, for pity's sakes!

A whispering, bustling group of gallerygoers cut off her view of Henry. In fact, they surrounded her, enfolding her as thirty or more of them swept into the room. One of them, who sounded vaguely like a street preacher with raspy, steamy voice, began a litany. His tale told of Holbein and how he'd been commissioned by Henry to paint and paint and paint.

Clare thought she'd faint. They pressed, they squeezed to hear their leader. So sequestered was she that she could not even rise from the bench. Suffocating, she stopped struggling and waited . . . and waited.

They drifted slowly, too slowly, around the circumference of the room.

But Clare was mesmerized and could not move.

Something held her spellbound. Something kept her seated, perspiring and breathing in little wisps of air.

She stuck a finger in the eyelet edging of her high-necked dress. Gad, if she could just get a good breath, she could think and —

"Clare!" Mirinda sank to her knees before her twin. "What's wrong?" She helped Clare undo the first two pearl buttons at her throat.

"Can't breathe," Clare managed to say, and tore off her prim shepherdess hat of Italian straw. "So warm."

"Oh, God. You are not going to faint, do you hear me? I will run to get help."

"No, no! Indy, come back." When Mirinda returned, her eyes wildly searching her twin's face, Clare smiled weakly. "I am not going to faint. I — I am physically very well. I simply had another vision." She gulped and shook her head as she felt Indy squeeze her fingers in compassion. "Not a vision, but a sensation." She chuckled. "Just as you predicted."

Mirinda had no idea if she should laugh or cry. She had never seen Clare like this. "I am going to find the Baron out in front and have him hail a hansom to take us home. You stay here until I return."

"Yes, that is best."

Clare watched her sister go through the marble columns and turn for the stairs. The only thing she had to do now was hold the sensation, hold it — and later understand it.

Eternities later, the two of them sat in the confines of the coach. The horse clip-clopped toward Mayfair and Clively Close, while Clare felt Mirinda's eyes upon her.

"I am quite well," Clare said. "I know you will want to put me to bed with lavender towels and tons of tea, but it is true. I am quite well."

"Shaken."

"By my own perceptions, yes." Clare turned her eyes to view the passing sights of midday London, then once more fastened them on her sister. "This time it was not a vision."

Mirinda sat quite still. "No?" She gulped. "What then?"

Clare considered her twin. She knew what Indy thought. Knew it not because she was perceptive, but because she was Indy's twin, her other self incarnate. Mirinda thought Clare was teetering on the edge of other more disastrous things.

"I smelled something."

That smartened Indy up. "Smelled what?"

Clare let her eyes drift closed. Let the aroma return. The feeling of being boxed up, closed in, swallowed her up . . . and then the voices came.

"What the hell do you mean she simply came in? Are you crazed?" seethed a low, hissing male voice.

"Not *me!*" crowed Ballantine so loud she could hear him plainly through the war chest. "It's *you!* You told me she knew more than she should."

"I told you because I thought you should take heed to be careful. I didn't mean for you to take it on yourself to poison her, for Christsakes! Now the police will want to know what happened to her. If you had let her go, we would be clear of suspicion."

"If we'd let her go, we'd be sitting in the local precinct — or worse, down in the cellar at the Foreign Office, where they keep the secret rooms you told me about."

"Nah! What's the use to talk to you? You never listen to reason. Now they will be coming for her and you'll let her free."

"Like hell, I will."

227

"Like hell, I say you will."

"No!"

It was then she had heard it. Then she had smelled it. Exactly what she had smelled today.

Clare opened her eyes to look at her worried sister. "When Mr Ballantine met his death yesterday, I heard him die. Heard the argument with his assailant. Heard him choking as the life was wrung from him directly over that box. But I also smelled an aroma. A cologne of spice and sandalwood mixed with leather and horse. Distinctive. I smelled it again today."

Mirinda had tears in her eyes and a smile on her lips. "And I would hope you would be able to remember it should you encounter it ever again?"

"No doubt about it."

"That's what I thought." She reached across the coach to squeeze Clare's hands. "Saturday will be your chance, you know."

"That was my thought, too. Not since Prince Bertie's wedding to Alexandra has there ever been such a gathering of notables and unnotables under one roof as there'll be at Julia and Dominik's wedding."

"If ever there was a chance to smell half of England, it will be there."

Twenty

The half of England Indy had predicted would attend the Clively-Swinford wedding today all had one thing in common: Each of them had bathed before he or she arrived.

Clare tucked into the wedding breakfast before her with more frustration than appetite. She had smelled as many of them as she could at the church and before the wedding party took their places on the dais here in the Marquess of Severn's grand ballroom in Belgravia.

But try as she might, she had sniffed no one of any import.

Clare sipped her Chablis and considered her task. Formidable, formidable. To smell half of England, one had to have great skill—and a clear head. Well, there was nothing for it, she would have to curtail her consumption of this excellent wine and wait until after breakfast to do her duty. Gus, who with the Baron had found no other clues to her man, was depending on her.

Her eyes roamed to the dais. And the jubilant bride.

Of the four sets of twins in the Clively family, Clare could think of none who appeared more dissimilar than Julia Mary and her sister Florence Catherine. Clare sat amazed. Why, the very way Julia ate — gobbling down her roast pigeon, apple stuffing, and creamed sherried biscuits — distinguished them.

Clare watched her young cousin, resplendent and wide in her white wedding satin and Valenciennes lace, and wondered how two twins could be so very different.

Where Julia was pudgy, Flo was fit, firm, and appealingly full in the bosom.

Where Julia was traditional and had wanted forever only a husband, Flo was unconventional, scandalizing her mother Honoria when she insisted upon taking up nursing with the Nightingales.

The truest test came a few months ago after the discovery of that body in the chimney. Where Julia was anxious to hide the discovery and secure the marriage contracts, Flo had blithely chuckled and joined Indy and Clare in their investigation. Of course, Julia had whined she might lose her big Scottish salmon of an Earl if he truly thought one of the Clivelys had actually killed that poor baby in the carriage house chimney!

Flo had worried one night in Clare's and Indy's presence that Julia would do anything — *anything* — to ensure the Earl took her to wife.

"I hope she has thought this through," Flo had said, truly worried about a woman who usually didn't merit such concern. "If she does what I think she suggests . . . well, I wonder if he finds the merchandise not up to his expectations, that he would really press on. I think Julia can be such a prig sometimes, but she is my sister and I don't want her to be a laughingstock."

230

Flo need not have worried. Julia got her man. Whatever she had or had not done, as merchandise, Julia had passed the Earl of Berwick's test. And actually, as Clare thought about it, she rather liked the man.

Clare raised her glass to her lips and tasted the wine's delicate sweetness as her eyes went to Dominik Swinford. Not a bad sort, really.

Fifty-seven years of age with all the lean, spare agility of a sportsman, he was an avid hunter, cricket player, and tennis player. He was not hard to look at, not with all that curly brown hair that grayed at the temples. He even had kind eyes, hazel ones to be exact. What's more, he had perfect, absolutely *perfect,* straight, white, bright teeth! She couldn't have carved them any straighter, brighter, whiter than this! The result was he had a captivating smile, and thus, if she were Julia, she might find much to enjoy about the Earl other than his large, legendary purse.

As for his legendary need for a male heir to his wealth from the Berwick Arms and Armament Foundry, he and the rest of the world would soon see if Julia could provide that little addition. Throughout the courtship, Julia certainly had played up to him enough, flirting with him with as little decorum as society permitted without fainting dead away. Even now, she looped her hefty satin-clad arm through Dominik's while he spoke with his best friend at his left, John Newhall. Gad, Julia could coo!

Cringing, Clare turned away and smiled at Mirinda, sitting at another circular table across the ballroom. Indy had been seated between Charles Beaumont and Gus.

Clare knew that that was Lucy's doing. Lucy, who

tried so diligently to pair guests with those they knew. Lucy, who as the eighth Marchioness of Severn, sought to do her duty a little too assiduously.

At the moment, Lucy sat next to her husband, Paul, on the dais with the newly married couple and the rest of the sixteen-member wedding party. For months, she had worked as hard as the mother of the bride and the bride herself.

Yesterday, Lucy had personally supervised the trimming of the grand ballroom of the Clively London residence Cotscombe with orange blossoms and lilies twined with pink and white ribbons. Last month, she had concocted the sumptuous menu, with Honoria's and Julia's instant approval, and hired the sedate string quartet. In April, she had ordered up from the family estate at Severna the richest of the family table linens, its silver, china, and crystal to serve each of the two hundred fifty guests now dining in her Belgravia house. And in the process, Lucy, whom Aunt Pru suspected carried the next Marquess of Severn, looked as though she had quite worn herself out for this social event of season.

Her husband, Paul, submerged as usual in his ruminations over his experiments with artificial insemination and genetic discoveries, seemed not to notice. Indeed, Clare wondered if his good wife of ten years had told him yet!

But Clare had in mind to tell Paul a few other things. And as the guests seemed to be finished with their repast, Lucy rose, giving the signal to the rest of the wedding party that they might now mingle with their guests.

Clare excused herself from her table and her partner, the wizened, widowered octogenarian M.P. for

Crewe, and made for her cousin Paul. Not having seen him since their birthday musicale two weeks previously, she admired how rested he looked after his extended trip to South America.

"Good morning, Clare!" Paul kissed her cheek and clasped her hands. "How stunning you look! A new gown?"

She nodded. "I couldn't resist when my dressmaker showed me this bolt of sapphire sicilienne."

"The rental of the townhouses proceeds, then?" he asked, his brown eyes soft with compassion and gentle inquiry.

"Yes, we have new tenants for Number Eighteen. Perhaps you know them, a newly married couple, Mr Charles Minton and his wife Diana?"

"Wonderful. I am delighted for you and Mirinda. I feared for your venture, what with the problem the evening of your musicale."

"Yes, quite. That seems to be proceeding apace," she lied. "What I did want to discuss with you was the parrot."

"Yes." Paul hooked his fingers in his vest pockets and rocked back on his heels, pleased with himself. "Like him, don't you?"

"As a matter of fact, I find him rather—"

Paul leaned forward, his dark eyes twinkling, his full lips grinning.

"Outrageous."

"Noo!" Paul leaned back, his portly stomach protruding, his chin tucked into his short, stocky neck. "I thought he would delight you!"

She tried to smile but knew it looked pained. "He is unpredictable. Sleeping, always sleeping. Then, when one least expects it, he begins blabbering.

233

And what he says, well! . . ."

"Yes," Paul nodded, scratching his graying side-burns. "I thought that would appeal to you."

Did she dare ask why? No. "I do wonder why he acts that way. Do you suppose he is ill? I mean, do birds sleep that much?"

"I doubt if they do in the jungle. The need to catch the next meal, you see. But I could take a look at him."

Him. Definitely him. Hmmm. "Could you?" How could she ask Paul to take him to Severna, when he seemed so delighted with his perfect gift? She couldn't.

"I would be happy to do so. He may simply be adjusting to his new home."

"Yes, well, it is his vocabulary that makes me wonder if his previous homes were very good ones. Do you know much about him?"

"Only that I won him in a horse race."

"Pardon me?"

"I won him as part of a prize when I bet in a private horse race. The gentleman who turned him over with the cash prize said the bird was very valuable."

"Why?"

"Why is he valuable? Good question. The man seemed so convinced, I hated to question him. The bird is rare."

"I will agree with that! Rarely awake. And when so, rarely civil."

Paul's oval face collapsed into his jowls. "Oh, dear, I am so sorry. I meant him to bring you joy. As soon as I heard his raucousness, I said to myself, 'Clare needs someone like this.' "

She did? Was she maudlin? Was she morose? She

was not certain. But Paul was so sweet about it all, she did not have the heart to argue. Then again, perhaps until her birthday, she *had* been all of those hideous things.

"Thank you, Paul. Perhaps, I should reconsider and—and train him."

"There's the spirit, Clare." He patted her on her back. "I knew you would find him amusing."

Amusing? Now she really was pained when she smiled at him.

Aunt Pru sailed to their side. "Good morning, Paul. Lovely send-off for our Julia. So nice of Lucy to offer Cotscombe. Good morning, Clare. I see you are looking fit. And your new gown is divine. A certain colour to your cheeks again. That is very good. Must be the attention you have received lately, eh?"

Clare demurred, hoping Paul would not take up this thread of conversation. He so liked matchmaking. And besides, Aunt Pru knew nothing of Tuesday's little sail down the Thames. "I do feel much better, thank you, Aunt. The summer air, you know."

"Yes. I should like to see even more roses in your cheeks, my dear. Perhaps a stay at the seaside would be a bracer, hmmm?"

"That sounds lovely."

Aunt Pru sipped her wine and winked at Clare. "We shall go, then. I have received a kind invitation from Dominik to go to his home at Cowes for a few weeks."

Paul nodded. "A wonderful idea. He and Julia are off to the Continent for two months, so his house is vacant there."

"Does Indy know?" Clare asked, unsure if her sister would care to go.

Paul snorted. "A foolish waste if she doesn't."

A foolish waste if she does—and Gus is gone when she returns.

Paul excused himself as one of his friends introduced another.

Aunt Pru cocked an eyebrow at Clare. "You will go, then?"

"Certainly. Why wouldn't I?"

"I wondered about your current social calendar. Mirinda tells me you have quite a few engagements—some with Gus's Baron von Macht, as well as with John Newhall. Perhaps you are too popular to take away from the London scene, my dear."

"In August? For Cowes? Aunt Pru, I would have to be engaged to the richest man alive before I failed to go to the seaside!"

"Exactly my thought, too."

Clare caught the eye of a passing waiter and asked her aunt if she cared for another glass of Paul's excellent French Chablis. "If you will allow me to walk you over to Freddie Matheson, Aunt, I must do the rounds of those I have not yet seen."

"Certainly." Aunt Pru took up a glass from the man's silver tray. "I cannot stop you from circulating here if I intend to whisk you away to Cowes, now, can I?"

Clare gave her aunt a quelling moue. But she had work to do. People to smell.

And, of course, she knew the ones she had not yet sniffed and must. Those from Gus's intimate circle. Those who would have received that handwritten note of his the other day. None of them had she been close enough to yet this morning. And all of them, each of them, she must now sniff with grace and precision.

Leslie Maccarran stood talking in one corner with

Charles Beaumont's wife, Brilliantine. Clare had not seen either, of course, since last Saturday evening at Gus's dinner party. Yet, she noticed that at her approach, the tall red-haired Scotsman and the dusky Gallic beauty seemed irritated. Clare stepped close, and as she passed pleasantries back and forth with them, she noticed that pouty Brilliantine smelled like lilacs and Leslie Maccarran like heather.

Clare sailed on.

Past Jocelyn Singleton, who smelled distinctly like his horse. Past Sir Joshua Sommes, who smelled faintly of tobacco and, oddly, so did his voluptuous wife Amarylis.

Clare then insinuated herself into a conversation with Petro Saldahna and her cousin Robin Clively. Though it took her a good ten minutes to decide Robin smelled like fine herb soap, Petro Saldahna definitely and irrevocably smelled like strawberries.

"Good morning, Clare," said Gus, who stood with Charles Beaumont and John Newhall. "Lovely wedding, did you not think so?"

"Yes, lovely." She was discreetly sniffing. "The bride is stunning. A Parisian gown," she was blathering on, probably sounding as silly as her parrot. Sliding as close as society would allow, she smiled at each of the men in turn and wondered that too many bodies pressed so closely together gave off such heat — and such a mix of odours!

Gus rattled on with inanities. Clare smiled and nodded, unable to comment for all of her constant, concealed sniffing.

Gus smelled faintly of cloves and cinnamon. No wonder Indy loved the man. He smelled better than many a pie Clare had ever eaten.

But Charles smelled definitely of pine and sandalwood. She needed to be closer to detect if the sandalwood was the same sort of essence she had smelled in the factory the other day, but he and Gus, joined by Brilliantine and Leslie Maccarran, turned off into their own little grouping.

John Newhall bent his head to her. "I understand you are going to Cowes."

Distressed at their departure, she had to laugh at John, who played the suitor to the hilt. "Who told you? Dominik?"

John shot up a rakish eyebrow. "No. Actually, *I* told him."

"You didn't!"

"I am with the Sommes's three houses along the shore during the very same time. I thought it might be a wonderful opportunity for me to show you the wonders of the yachting season. Bertie is there at that time of year and — I say, you look odd. What is wrong, Clare?"

The distinct smell of sandalwood floated past her and into her mind. This was it. This was the smell. It brought back memories and weakness.

John grabbed for her elbow. "You look faint. Let's take you out for some air."

She gladly went with him, gladly leaned on him, gladly welcomed his sturdier arm round her waist once they were outside among the early roses on the front lawn.

"You look rather green, my dear," he said soothingly.

"I feel rather ugly," she murmured, and tried to push back the revulsion that surged at the sandalwood.

238

"I say I had better take you home. Come now, don't argue."

She didn't. She couldn't. She simply sat amid the saccharine-sweet roses while he hailed a hansom from across the street. She was grateful, so grateful, when he assisted her up and inside. She sank into the squabs. And then when he joined her, sitting next to her, and put his arm about her to draw her close, Clare surrendered her head to his chest.

And in the next moment, she drew it up and away.

She stared at him.

So handsome, so dignified, so distinguishable from all his colleagues because he, of them all, smelled of sandalwood and spice.

"Oh, my God," she muttered. "It was you in that factory Tuesday, wasn't it, John?"

His expression fell from concerned to appalled.

She sniffed again. No doubt about it.

This was her man. Her nemesis. Her murderer.

Twenty-one

"Remove your clothes, I say!"

Clare clutched at the bodice of the sapphire gown she'd had made especially for this day. If John Newhall thought he could abscond with her and try to kill her, that was one thing. But to endure the ruin of yet another new gown because of his willfulness was quite another. "I will not."

"Then I will have my woman tear it from you," he said, nodding to the tall Chinese maidservant who stood in the corner of the library in John's quaint Kensington townhouse.

The dark, silent Chinese woman in red flowing robes advanced, and Clare retreated to the wall. As the woman's long-nailed fingers reached for her, Clare shrank into the leather-bound volumes. "I will not have this. It is too undignified."

"Ah, my dearest Clare," John advanced, his once-pleasant gray eyes now narrow slits of impatience, "dignity is precisely what one does not need when one is dead."

She shivered at this transformation of John Newhall from gentleman to devil. "How can you kill me?" she asked in that contralto voice that made many a man consider her a second time. "I was one you were interested in as —"

"That day has come and gone. Take your gown off, Clare, and put on this robe." He held out one plain muslin wrap, the sort criminals were buried in.

"Where did you get that?"

"Does it matter? You'll wear it, my dear, so that if anyone finds your body, they never discover your identity."

She gulped. How could a man go from suitor to killer in so short a time? Clare had always been a better judge of character than that. Where had she failed to perceive this? How? "You do mean to kill me."

His patrician hand cupped her cheek as he raised her face to peer into her eyes. "Never doubt it, my dearest. I wish I did not need to, but I do. You would never forget what I have done and, sorry to say, never forgive it, either."

Clare sidestepped the greedy fingers of the Chinese maid. "Tell me why, John. Tell me why you did it, and I will do as you ask and come quietly."

"Quietly? Clare, you shrieked so loud in the hansom they heard you in Dover."

"One does not put a gun to a lady's rib cage in midday, sir, and expect the lady to accept it as her due."

"Remove the gown, and I will enlighten you."

She nodded and began with her Belgian straw bonnet with the giant turquoise blue faille ribbons and stunning blue feathers. Upon his maroon leather chair, she tenderly laid the hat that had cost her a choice between oysters for luncheon or mere codfish. Clare sighed. No hats or oysters from now on. "I cannot believe you are a killer. And so sordid a means, too."

His lean face was stark, his lean body calm, determined. "I had no choice. The man saw me. Knew who

I was."

"You mean he saw you in the park?"

"Yes. Go on"—he wiggled a few fingers—"remove your gown."

She reached for her earbobs. Grandmother Howard's sapphires. "But you were with Señor Saldahna when you left, and Charles, too, if I remember."

"Petro took a carriage with Charles Beaumont. My good fortune, too, that when the Dawes brothers interrogated Charles and Petro, they forgot to ask if I had climbed into the carriage with them."

She placed her earbobs on a walnut reading table and wondered how efficient those Dawes boys were. But then to castigate them was nothing to how she castigated herself for unprocessed facts. "Why did you not join them? Did you see Lo-wu waiting there in the park?"

"No. It is all your fault, my dear Clare."

"Mine?" She stood stunned. "How could that be?"

"My mind was full of you. I have wanted you, you see, for many years. Just as I have wanted other things I could not possess."

She reached for the clasp of her sapphire and pearl necklace and paused. "I do not understand."

"No. I am positive you wouldn't. You see, I went walking to think. To plan."

"But my footman?" she asked more of herself than of John. Burton had been posted outside. Why had he not seen or heard the commotion? Burton . . .

"Was nowhere to be seen. The park was still. Dark."

"Where was he?" She remembered, too late, how nervous Burton had been that morning after the murder when she and Indy had questioned him. In all the rush of events—births and weddings and sailing down the Thames—she had forgotten to pursue what that nervousness truly meant.

"I have no idea what happened to him, nor do I care. I know he was not at his post. Fortunate for me."

"An excellent opportunity."

"Yes, a lovely evening to contemplate a liaison with a lovely lady. Yes, I considered you a catch, my dear. A prize. A beautiful, older, accomplished woman and one I should have had, had I the money. Yes, money. You are the sort of woman a man wishes for. Good family, good breeding. Good-tempered. But neither you nor anyone like you could ever be mine—not until now."

He groaned and wrung his hands together. "Now that is the irony. Because now that I have the money from my own private endeavours, I also have the position and prestige to live as I should have all along. And isn't it ironic, then, that the very evening when I see it come together I see it fall apart?" He tore at his hands. "My good God, how I hated him for taking that from me!"

"What did Lo-wu take from you? Goods?"

"Ha! Nothing so small. My goods"—John's hands swept the room—"he was welcome to. No. He knew of my operations. But what else he knew of me was worth more—my life and my reputation as the British emissary to China."

"You mean to say you think he traveled thousands of miles across the face of the earth to come here and meet a man to blackmail him?"

"No. He did not travel here to do it, but he did

243

when he saw me. I knew—or I should say, I deduced—why he was here in England, incognito as he was. Lo-wu was a famous Bannerman, head of the Imperial Guard, and many knew he loved the Yi Concubine from the time they were children. I had heard rumours she had gone missing from Tzu Hsi's massacre, and when I saw him there in the park, I had only to ask about her and he flinched. But then the next words from his mouth were about our mutual past. His next words were for money in return for silence. But because I knew his circumstances and what he faced here in England as a Chinese man alone, I expected him someday to ask for more money than I could give."

"Why, for heaven's sake? Was what he knew about so horrid that—"

"Yes, damn it!"

"What?" Clare advanced on him. "What could be so terrible?"

"I killed a man! A friend of his. Lo-wu was in Taku visiting him the day he died. Lo-wu saw me and Ballantine emerge from the man's house."

"My good God! *You* killed the Chinese official in the Taku incident! It is no surprise that no one was ever found. You were investigating a murder you yourself committed! How could you?!"

"You must know now that self-protection is the most important aspect of any endeavour. The old government official was selling me goods. He was part of my supply ring. I needed him, but one day he said he no longer needed me and that he would smuggle his goods past the *compradores* through another man. I needed my income from a smuggling ring it had taken me decades—yes, *decades*—to build. I had money,

244

enough of it for the first time in my life, and I was damned if I was going to give it up because of this old man's greed. Yes, I killed the man in Taku. It was easy to tell Charles there was no information in the British sector. Charles is so sensitive, it was easy to lure him."

"Charles Beaumont *knew* you had killed the official?"

"No. Poor devil knows nothing, except that his wife is a flirt and a consummate spender of every sou." He pointed a forefinger at her bodice. "The buttons, Clare."

She did as she was told. Knowing all the details made her sad. "So you saw Lo-wu, assumed he would continue to make trouble for you, and then you tied him up and killed him. How could you so cold-bloodedly do that to a man?"

"It was such quick work, I never contemplated it. My walking stick with its little dagger in the ivory handle was at hand. It was the first means of dispatch I thought of. It seemed so . . . appropriate. And Lo-wu was so surprised, he never gained any physical advantage.

"Besides, I knew someone would eventually discover who Lo-wu was and what *he* had smuggled into England. Emasculation seemed such a *Chinese* way to kill him that the Yard would blame the death to Tzu Hsi. But I never anticipated that someone would realize emasculation is not punishment for touching the emperor's concubine, decapitation is. I never anticipated that someone would be *you*."

"And I did not want to believe that someone I knew could do such a thing." Neither did Gus, who worried that any one of his once-trusted colleagues was a murderer, or worse, that all of them were in league in the crime.

"We make numerous mistakes in our lives. The worst are miscalculations of other people's characters. With you, I miscalculated three things: your knowledge of China, your persistence, and your courage. Rest assured, I shall never make those mistakes again."

He raised his chin, indicating she should continue to disrobe. And then he watched her, arms folded, eyes appreciative of what she revealed.

"I would have loved you, you know," John whispered as she opened the bodice and tugged at her lace-trimmed sleeves to shrug out of the entire affair. "You are a stunning woman," he said as his soulful eyes ate her up. "I needed an accomplished wife, for once. I would have done us both proud. This commission with Gus will last for years and years, you know. And I would have made you a good husband."

His gray eyes slid to hers as she stepped from her sapphire skirt. Clad now in her low-cut cambric chemise, crinoline, and bustle, she arched a brow.

"Christ, what you women wear. Take it off."

"I cannot."

"I said—"

"I am no contortionist to reach the back."

He motioned to the Chinese maid and said something in Cantonese, which Clare needed no knowledge of the language to understand.

The woman worked furiously against the complexities of ribbons at the waist, snaps at the bustle, more ribbons down the back, another layer of crinolette and petticoat. Finally, Clare stood defiantly in her pink coutil corset, her white silk stockings, and her pale cambric drawers.

With regret in his eyes, he surveyed Clare one last time, then turned to his maid with rapid-shot instructions.

John turned his back and the maid brought out a knife.

"No!" Clare fell back.

The Chinese maid wrestled with her, deftly slicing the corset from her. Clutching her bare bosom, Clare panted and worked her way around the edges of the wall.

The woman advanced on Clare, held out the sacque, and motioned for her to don it. Without argument, she did so, and within seconds, Clare felt her hands yanked behind her and bound. Without a backward glance, John began to open the double doors and leave the room.

Clare had to provoke him, save herself, anything to stop him and this woman! "You cannot escape, John."

He paused but did not turn around. "I will, Clare. I have escaped so much else all these years." He closed the doors with a snap.

The woman prodded Clare toward the hallway, the stairs, the cellar.

Clare took in every nook, every cranny, every door, every window.

How to get out?

How to go?

With the knife to Clare's back, the maid forced her down a dark, silent hallway in what should have been the servants' quarters.

But no one was about.

No one.

Clare despaired.

247

With a jerk to Clare's arms, the maid spun her about, forcing her through an empty kitchen, round an old oak table, and headed toward the door. The woman passed the pantry, thrust open the kitchen door, but never stepped out.

Mirinda had the woman round the neck, one butcher knife pointed straight at her jugular.

Clare started, shocked at being saved.

Mirinda pushed the woman toward a chair.

Outside, Clare could hear running feet, shouts, and the loud report of a gun.

Twenty-two

July 15, 1875

Clare and Mirinda watched the Severna coachman secure Yi-an's trunk to the tailrack of the massive vehicle. The sisters' eyes locked, each understanding that this was an ending to their journey and a beginning for the delicate lady who had come into their lives and touched each of them.

The lovely young woman, dressed in a lightweight ulster and one of Flo's altered walking suits, clutched Lee Davenport in a heartfelt hug. Between them Yi-an held her healthy baby boy. Above the head of this cooing child who should have been the emperor of the giant Middle Kingdom, Yi-an and her friend Lee Davenport spoke words that Mirinda and Clare understood with their hearts.

Each sister had already given the lovely lady her farewell of fond embrace and words of assurance that Paul and his very expectant wife Lucy would be the best of all possible employers and friends in Yi-an's time of need.

Now, as Yi-an accepted the footman's hand up into the Marquess of Severn's coach, Mirinda, Clare, and Lee formed a trio of waving well-wishers. Yi-an did nothing other than cry amid her grateful smile.

"Oh, God," said Mirinda as they moved off down Clively Circle. "I wish her well."

Clare hugged her sister's waist. "No one will find her in Severna. It is too far, too obscure a place for Tzu Hsi to seek the boy there."

Lee wiped tears from her eyes. "I have a feeling you are right, Clare. Tzu Hsi is bright, but she cannot search every square mile in the world for this child."

As the black coach turned off the Circle onto Scarborough Street, the three women waved again.

"Besides, Lee, Mirinda and I go to Severna often for visits and we will insist you come, too," said Clare.

"And I know Yi-an will be a great help to Lucy when the babies are born," said Mirinda.

Clare turned on her twin. "No! You don't really think Lucy would have twins, do you?"

"Of course, I do. What *else* do Clivelys have?"

Clare was nodding.

Lee was chuckling.

Indy glanced at Lee. "Will you come have tea with us?"

"Thank you, I would like that." The three fell into step along the walk to Scarborough House. "I felt so awkward when I had to hide things from you both. I was terrified and did not know what to do, whom to trust."

Clare took Lee's hand and squeezed it. "I can well understand that. England is so new to you, and then to have someone as important — and as dangerous — as Yi-an in your household must have been daunting."

The three turned up the walk for the front steps of Scarborough.

"Yes, it was. But you saved us all, Clare."

Indy grinned as she opened her front door for them. "Clare knew so much of China, only she could have solved the case. The Yard was astounded when Ian explained the sordid mess and they continue to be, even though they understand Gus's and Leslie Maccarran's explanation and the need to keep things mum, lest Tzu Hsi stir a typhoon of problems. Why, even our friend Ann Billings Wentworth saw the importance of never printing a word of the truth."

"Yes," mourned Clare as they stepped into Indy's vestibule and made for the conservatory, where they had told Hopkins to lay on a hefty teatime feast, "I agree I was instrumental in discovering it all. But I do wish I hadn't."

Lee put an arm around Clare's shoulder. "You liked John Newhall very much, didn't you?"

"Yes. And no."

The other two women looked puzzled as each sank into a chair round the octagonal table Hopkins had arranged for service.

"Dear sister, I think you must explain that remark to Lee and me."

"I liked him. I wanted to like him — perhaps too much. My desire to have a relationship overwhelmed good reason and made me miss so many details."

"Such as?" asked Indy as she began to pour for them all.

"I failed to pursue an inkling I had that Burton was evasive with us about his actions that night."

Indy mashed her lips together. "Clare, everyone must heed the call of nature when it comes. The poor boy had simply partaken of too much food and punch and had to seek out the privacy of the backyard between what he thought were normal carriage runs."

"Yes . . . well, I know about it now and it seems so normal. But I failed to follow up on it. Then, of course, there is the most important thing I failed to understand."

Indy handed over a teacup to Lee. "Whatever was that?"

"I tended to think of how nice John was instead of *who* could have had the opportunity to kill a man in our park. Obviously, the criminal was most likely to have been someone who either lived here or attended our party."

Indy tisked. "You must not castigate yourself, Clare. You had so many other things right, it was probably outrageous to contemplate one of our acquaintances actually emasculating a man. Even Gus could barely bring himself to think that of his friends and cohorts. And if Gus, who was trained to discern every nuance of every truth, cannot do it, you can be forgiven and forgive yourself." She gave Clare her tea.

"Thank you, Indy. You have always been my bulwark. And now I understand that I do not love John and never did, never could. I still feel badly about him, sitting in gaol, wounded and worried over his future."

Indy sat back in her chair. "He committed his foul deeds and he shall pay for them. Sad to see a man of his breeding in gaol, and sad to hear him rail against Gus and the Baron shooting him to stop his escape, but John took his chances and he lost. He lost, Clare. You must not grieve for a man who would not have grieved for you."

"Yes," said Lee. "He would have killed you, Clare, to save himself. He deserves no pity."

"Nothing at all, Clare," affirmed Indy. "He lead a

double life for years, robbing the Chinese government of its rightful taxes on goods he smuggled. What kind of example could that be for a diplomat, a man charged with making the best of international affairs? No, he deserves no pity, my dear. John Newhall was a criminal. And what you must do is forget him as he would have done so quickly with you."

Clare inhaled, relieved — and feeling freer with Indy's kind words and clear thinking. "I think I will welcome a few weeks at Cowes."

Mirinda smiled. She wanted Clare to continue to recuperate from that illness of hers. And she wanted Clare's company and counsel, particularly about this new seemingly permanent condition of having Gus about. But most of all, she was thrilled, joyous at the news that her sister was showing some of her innate spunk — especially for one of her favourite places, the seaside. "I am thrilled."

"Yes," said Clare, more to herself than the others. "And this time when I go sailing, I want to do it the right way!"

"The right way?"

"The last time I went sailing, I had a horrid view, terrible accommodations, nor was I suitably dressed for the occasion. This time, I will have my binoculars, Dominik Swinford's sumptuous home, and a few new frocks!"

Mirinda chuckled. "You are well recovered from all your troubles, Clare, when you once more wish to visit your dressmaker."

About The Author

ANN CROWLEIGH is the pseudonym for the brilliant and prolific writing team of Barbara Cummings and Jo-Ann Power. Both are residents of Maryland and members of Sisters in Crime and Malice Domestic. Look for their next CLIVELY CLOSE mystery, *Silence, Cold As Death,* in May 1994.

A former editor of two lifestyle magazines for the Washington, D.C. area, Barbara Cummings is a Rhode Island native. Jo-Ann Power has been as a reporter, teacher, and a public relations executive for a corporation and a national trade association. In addition to CLIVELY CLOSE, Barbara and Jo-Ann collaborate on contemporary women's fiction, written under their own names. RISKS is available this month from Pinnacle Books.

Barbara and Jo-Ann love to hear from their fans. Write to them, c/o Zebra Books, 475 Park Avenue South, New York, NY 10016.